# Praise for *Come Back, I Love You (A Ghost Story)*

"Kathleen Novak is a wise and resourceful author, and her fifth novel a pleasing blend of stranger-in-town trope, prose poetry, and ghost story. Set on a northern lake—as much a character as a landscape—an unnamed protagonist has abandoned her past for this tiny cottage in the middle of nowhere, her narrative teasing back and forth between a life once lived and the life she has now. Still waters run deep, and time has a funny way of slipping by. Novak knows this and delicately manages the reader's expectations and desires."

—Richard Peabody, editor, *Gargoyle Magazine*

"*Come Back, I Love You* is a lyrical, mystical tale of a woman's search for herself amid the ghosts of her past—and one she was not expecting."

Howard Owen, author of twenty-four novels, including *Littlejohn* and the *Willie Black* mystery series

"*Come Back, I Love You* is a poetic, gothic pentimento of leaving and finding home. Satisfying, lyrical, haunting, one of those can't-put-it-down reads. We never learn the narrator's true name, adding to the mystery. She might be any of us."

—Carolyn Colburn, author of *Morlocks in the Basement* and *Minimum Maintenance*

"With a voice as ethereal and luminous as the novel's subject, Kathleen Novak lulls the reader across the thin line between here and the hereafter, exploring how we show up for others—or don't, creating our own fleeting realities. Lakeside, summer—the story's lush setting is finely etched, masterfully evoking how a person's longing for a place is as strong as any love for a person. *Come Back, I Love You* is a marvel, leaving me to wonder that we may all be ghosts, merely passing through this hauntingly beautiful world."

—Margaret Hutton, author of *If You Leave*

"Here is a novel of easy warmth and great charm, dealing with love, loss, and a ghostly presence demanding attention."

—Faith Sullivan, author of *The Cape Ann* & many others

"An examination of death that is anything but elegiac, *Come Back, I Love You* is a poetical respite from the frenzy of life, an evocative contemplation, a paean to peace and tranquility."

—Chris Knopf, author of the *Sam Acquillo Hamptons Mysteries*

"Kathleen Novak writes skillfully about the human feelings—love, loneliness, ambivalence and fear—that shape her characters' lives, relationships, and ultimate destinies. *Come Back, I Love You* is a quiet, powerful novel."

—Dine Watson, author of *Transplant*, 2023 Washington Writers' Publishing House Nonfiction Prize winner

"Does everyone think they will return? the protagonist, who calls herself Floria, wonders in Kathleen Novak's captivating novel, *Come Back, I Love You.* There's so much heart in this book. For romantic loves, lost and found. For parents and grandparents. For elderly neighbors we've only just met. There's a sweetness here of the finest, non-cloying variety that sneaks up on you, leaves you rooting for our hero, and, finally, leaves you breathless."

—Andrew Furman, author of *Jewish* and *The World That We Are*

## Additional Praise for Kathleen Novak

"Eloquent, graceful prose sweeps the reader along in this immensely satisfying novel about choices that alter a life."

—*Publishers Weekly,* starred review, *The Autobiography of Corrine Bernard*

"The result is a taut and beguiling meditation on love, loss, secrets, and silences. Tender and intricately written, this well-crafted novel is poetic, evocative, and beautiful."

—*Kirkus Reviews, Do Not Find Me*

"*Do Not Find Me,* written by a Minneapolis-based author raised on the Iron Range, is so stunning in its beautiful writing, you will want to read it twice, just to savor her poetic talents."

—Mary Ann Grossman, *Pioneer Press*

"Novak's *Steel* holds enormous weight…a story that rolls like an ore train picking up steam."

—Aaron Brown, *Mesabi Tribune*

Other books by Kathleen Novak

*Do Not Find Me*

*Rare Birds*

*The Autobiography of Corrine Bernard: A Novel*

*Steel*

# Come Back, I Love You (A Ghost Story)

Kathleen Novak

Regal House Publishing

Published by
Regal House Publishing, LLC
Raleigh, NC 27605


ISBN -13 (paperback): 9781646036561
ISBN -13 (epub): 9781646036578
Library of Congress Control Number: 2024951349

Cover images and design by © studiochi.art



Printed in the United States of America

Regal House Publishing, LLC
https://regalhousepublishing.com

for June
wherever you are

It’s all the same
what we say to the traveler,
the dying, the madwoman:
Come back, I love you, come back.

—from “Heedless” by Penelope Austin

# 1

## Cabbage Roses

I did not plan to leave.

Nor did I leave for any one reason.

It was the accumulation, the disappointments and failings, those who died and those who drifted. Certainly, I did not leave for lack of a story. There is always a story. One thing follows another and that is the story. But it wasn't the story I had envisioned. Let's say the plot faltered, characters remained stubbornly independent, pages wore with the effort.

I pulled the lens back far enough to blur my horizon and I left.

Now I have paid in full for a seven-hundred-some-square-foot cottage on a narrow strip of land, from winding road above to weedy lakeshore below. The realtor calls it a find. It needs a little work and a little paint, but what's that, she says. A few bucks at the hardware store.

It's old, this lakeside cottage, built in 1902, and purchased shortly after by a couple who lived here the rest of their lives. They put a porch on two sides and papered the walls with a tumble of pink roses, which they also planted all around the house. Cabbage roses, the realtor tells me. Heirloom, no less.

When these owners died, the cottage was bequeathed to their family, all too old now to care. It didn't sell immediately. My realtor says there is not enough land for building anything anyone would want. I have a stone fireplace across one wall and archways instead of doors and heavy curtains that separate the bedrooms. The kitchen is the size of a dime. At least it has a foundation, the realtor affirms. You won't blow away in a tornado. Like Dorothy.

Though the cottage has been emptied of furniture, some

art remains on the walls, three small oil paintings depicting the seaside and small boats at sea and a wide empty beach at the edge of the sea. In every painting the sky is growing dark and each has at least one spot of the brightest red—the hull of a sailboat, a woman's dress on the beach, the roof of a house far off in the distance. They have hung here for years, apparently, with their vision of shore and sea.

The lake outside my door, however sprawling and deep, is not the sea. Still, I hear the cries of gulls, catch glimpses of them soaring. I doubt they know the difference between a deep lake and an ocean and if they do, what do they care? Like me, they are on their own wherever they are.

Everything inside my cottage is covered with dust or grit and cleaning takes me all day. The delivery men set things up, place my chairs and heavy oak table in the middle of the room. I have taken only my favorite belongings, which is another part of the leaving. Paring down, editing. My kitchen is now three old pans and two very sharp knives, a few baking tins, and the dishes my mother bought when my parents were first married. They're not fine china, but that's how she used them. She bought twelve place settings, allowing her to have both her siblings and their children for dinner, though I struggle to remember if that ever happened. This also allowed three tables of bridge, which I remember happening regularly, the house filled with perfumes of the day, Evening in Paris and Miss Dior.

I've made up my bed in heavy cotton sheets my grandmother trimmed with her handmade lace, sheets I've saved for decades, almost too exceptional for ordinary sleep. But now I like having my grandmother with me. I like thinking of her hands, always smoothed by rosewater and glycerin, working with her silver tatting shuttle, proficient enough to make lace and watch *As the World Turns* at the same time.

I like having all of them with me, anyone whose long-gone presence hovers here whenever I want and wanes whenever I want. I don't speak to them but they speak to me. My father tells me to replace the bent-out screens or I'll have flies all summer.

My mother recommends I polish these rough wooden floors.

The bedroom is one of two nooks off the main room, both separated by heavy chintz of an earlier vintage. It's a beautiful sight, the small lamp on my bedside table, my grandmother's sheets on the bed, and after I turn off the light, I lie still, hands folded on top of the lace hem. These flowers on the wallpaper remind me of the cabbage roses that have not yet bloomed outside. I suppose they will open in tight layers like cabbages do, though I know only roses sold by florists and those my mother coaxed up a trellis against my childhood home. There have been no cabbage roses in my story until now.

Beyond my windows the lake rolls and recedes on the shore.

I should plant cabbages too. I should plant a cabbage for every rose.

# 2

## What & Where & Who

For a few days here I've had much to do to settle, no rush, no schedule, no commitment to anyone anywhere. When I decided to move, I packed in a hurry. Now I unwrap items from a lifetime as though I've never seen them before, the surprising aspect of time on my side. The soft air. The lake beyond my door.

I cannot see my neighbors. To the south, the lot is enormous with a wooded area providing privacy and distance. Sometimes voices echo off the water and I'll hear a boat idling, but I do not see the people who live there. To the north I am separated by a thicket of bushes. A weathered gray roof shows above and, now and then, I catch sight of a small black dog racing about.

I've spent three days in silence and am moving toward my third night falling asleep to the easy sound of water against shore. Near dusk I put on Puccini's *La Tosca.* I saw it at the Metropolitan Opera House in New York and again at the Royal Opera House in London and, to some degree, I return to those places every time I hear the music. I sort my books, totally absorbed, and so do not hear that someone is at the door until a voice calls out, "Oh my, I didn't think anyone would ever move in here." A round, white-haired woman, dog at her side, peers through the porch screen. "I'm Maeve Murphy from next door," she says, "and this is Eddie."

I go to greet her, and Maeve Murphy hands me a loaf of warm banana bread. "Oh my," she says again. "I never thought anyone would move in here. How delightful it is. My children wanted me to buy this place for the land, but I don't need any more land. I'm perfectly happy with what I have over there. Goodness, how delightful this is."

I ask if she'd like to sit down, but she does not. The sun is beginning to set and Puccini fills the room. "Just came to say hello," she says. "Happy to have a neighbor, aren't we, Eddie? Don't worry about him. He's just the best dog, a rescue. You know they are always so grateful, but Eddie's the best. A gentleman, my daughters say." She remains by the door. "Are you alone?"

I say that I am, that I have moved here to live more simply. By a lake. Minding my own business, I say, and I see the flicker of recognition. "That's just what I did when my Jim died," she responds. "We had a big house, eight children. My husband was a doctor and when he died, everyone had an opinion about what I should do. Come live with me, Mother, buy a condo in the city, Mother. At first I didn't even want to sell my house. It was my life, that house, so it took a while to get going. I decided to live in a high-rise condominium on the banks of the river, which sounds fine I suppose." She stops to call Eddie back to her side. "But I just couldn't think of myself walking down a hallway to home, you know what I mean? Anyway, I bought my rambler here and got Eddie for company. It's been seven years and things are just fine, they're just fine. Though I must say I got cheery when I saw you moving in."

"Well, it's nice to meet you," I say, and this is true.

"Did you tell me your name? I'm so forgetful. Wait until you're old and you'll know what I mean."

I have no plan for who I am or want to be. *La Tosca* is in its third act, anguish rising powerfully. "I'm Floria," I answer. I repeat it, Floria, give no last name.

"Beautiful! What your mother must have been thinking when she named you that."

"It's from an opera."

"Oh, and that's beautiful too. My husband and I never thought to name any of our children after characters in opera. Are you always called Floria or may I call you Florie? No, never mind, Floria's such a beautiful name." Eddie's tail wags the whole time she talks.

"Let me know if you need anything, Floria. I'm glad to have you here." She and Eddie leave just as the sun drops across the lake. I stand on my porch and watch them make their slow way back through the bushes to their own house where, within minutes, the lights go on.

Sitting in one of the deep wooden chairs on my porch, I listen and watch for a long time, waiting for nothing to happen. I hadn't intended to rename myself after a tragic figure, hadn't intended to rename myself at all. The music has ended now and I am still holding Maeve Murphy's banana bread, the aroma as familiar as the moths fluttering against my screens.

# 3

## Whirry Little Road

The kitchen cupboards here are lined with old newspapers, red thumbtacks holding them in place along the edges. The first few I pull off are from 1962, advertising Ford Falcons and Chevrolet trucks, Motorola cabinet televisions, Oleo at ten cents a pound, even Teeth Extractions Without Pain. Early on my husband and I lived in a lower duplex built by a Swedish couple who stayed there all their lives, like the owners of this cottage. The cupboards in that apartment also reached to the ceiling and had yellowed newspapers lining the shelves.

I used to picture that previous owner—a tiny woman, I decided, with the sky-blue eyes that many Swedish people have and thin hair pulled back as best she could. I can't say why I saw her like that, and always in a housedress a bit too big for her, one of her husband's leather belts pulled tight enough around her to give the dress some shape. She wore the type of shoes my grandmother wore, black lace-ups, perforated for the circulation of air and open at the toe for comfort. Shoes for doing the wash and weeding the yard as well as walking to town to shop. My husband thought my level of detail on this suspicious. Had I seen her floating through our house? He thought those kinds of things. We both thought those things. But I did not see the Swedish woman except in my imagination.

I'm still working when the realtor's rusted Mercedes convertible comes down the drive. "Hallo? You here?" She teeters toward the back door in her three-inch heels, swinging a white paper bag. "I've got donut holes," she calls. "The best you'll ever eat."

I step outside and there she is as ever, hair in place, her long nails painted red. "Listen," she goes on, "I just heard from the seller and she said to tell you the paintings she left were done by her mother-in-law, the one who lived here forever. She used to win prizes at the State Fair. Thought I should tell you. Not that they're valuable or anything, but she forgot to say that before. If I'd known earlier, I might have jacked up the price a bit." She laughs, showing an accidental smudge of lipstick on her teeth. "This business, right? You never know." Then she tells me the donut holes are a specialty and if you don't get to that bakery before nine in the morning they're all gone.

I offer her one, but she declines on the grounds of watching her figure. This, too, she thinks funny and walks back to her car laughing. She peels out back up to the road, dirt spitting from her tires, and a pleasant stillness settling in her wake.

I love the sounds of morning on this lake. And the smells, the sense that things are fresh, moist, fluid. The calls of birds are magnified. There is always some kind of breeze rustling the leaves, the roll of water constant, the light of any hour reflected on its surface. I circle the cottage barefoot, eat a couple of the donut holes still warm, the glaze melting. I don't have a dock and the shore is not the best, but I step into the water anyway, breaking off chunks of donut hole for an eager gull on shore. Then, instead of returning to my cupboards, I find my shoes and head to the road for a walk.

I've been a walker since I was old enough to wander the streets of my hometown at night. After supper, my mother would retreat with a book and my father to putter in the garage, neither concerned that I disappeared into the dark of evening. Their lack of worry interests me now, but at the time I took it for granted.

I can measure entire eras of my life by walks I took. Once, the length of Manhattan in the rain. At a corner store on the Upper East Side, I bought a black umbrella with a wooden handle which I use to this day. That was when I discovered a Hungarian bakery, the two women behind the counter dressed in crisp white, their English halting, endearing, and I bought a pastry, the name of which I have since forgotten. There was a beach in Southern California where I walked once a month for a decade. I stayed in an old-moneyed hotel across the railroad tracks and up a slight hill from the ocean—a place where high rollers came for the horse racing seasons and well-dressed women came to lunch. Around six in the morning I'd hear the first train go through heading north to Los Angeles. I'd make my way to the coastline, sometimes still blackened by the tide, and I'd stride along close to the sea, its roar defying any troubles on my mind at the time.

I could go on and on. I've traveled much, often on my own, and everywhere I went I wanted to walk.

Walking was something the women in my childhood did, a freedom they had. My mother walked nearly every day of her life. As she aged she had knee problems and heart problems and a constant ache in her back. But she never stopped walking. She walked the day she died.

For fifty-some years my grandmother and her best friend walked to the movies on Sunday afternoons. They'd make their way along the four blocks to downtown, stopping to face one another whenever they had something to say, a garden to discuss, a story to tell. Then they'd continue. The pace never mattered. If they arrived in the middle of the first matinee, they would stay until the middle of the second.

This grandmother was always an influence. Hers are the sheets I sleep under in my new life. The day I left for school in the city, she stood on the porch of her house and waved and waved, her eyes as sad as the end of the road. *Bye-bye. I meana go slow*, she said with her familiar Italian accent. She'd started life on a mountain tending sheep, making lace while the animals grazed around her. She witnessed horses giving way to cars and the invention of radio, which then gave way to television and on that television, she saw rockets launched and Neil Armstrong walking on the moon. She was the one to hold my hand, make popcorn, tell stories in the dark. That's why she stays with me. Cocking her head just so. *I meana go slow.*

I do not know how far I walk today and it does not matter. There are more cars on the road than I expected and little shade. I kick back down my pebbled driveway thinking I may have to find somewhere else near my cottage to ramble. When I spot lavender-blue flowers growing wild on my hill, I pick a few and arrange them in a juice glass.

Then on a whim, I make my way through the bushes to Maeve Murphy's yard.

# 4

## Portrait Of A Neighbor

"Floria—for heaven's sake come in," Maeve says at the door. "Excuse the clutter. I've always got too much going here." A baby grand piano takes up half her living room, the dining table is covered in papers, typewriter open, a cut-glass bowl of fresh fruit in the middle. "Harebells! Now where did you find harebells? I suppose they're all over and I haven't even noticed."

"I picked them along my driveway. I didn't know what they were called."

"How nice, Floria. Thank you." She says she'll make us some tea, keeps moving about her kitchen as she talks. "I'm so glad you came over. I wanted to check in on you but my kids tell me I talk too much, so I let you be. At least for a few days," she adds. "It's such a nice little place you have there. Well, here we go." She hands me the tea tray, my bouquet in the middle, and we shuffle out onto her deck facing the lake.

She sighs as she lowers into the chair, her movements stiff. "Perfect," she says. "I'm so glad you came by. I like a little neighborly company. When our kids were small, Jim and I bought a cabin and that's where we went every summer. Families all around, people in and out of each other's places, always sand on the floors. Such fun, such a good time of life. But out here, people tend to keep to themselves."

"Even so, it's busier than I expected on the road."

"Tell me," she says. "Of course, my children don't want me to drive anymore at all, but I can't live out here and not drive. How would we get dog biscuits, right, Eddie?" He sits at her feet, glances up at the mention of his name.

"You need a dog, Floria. A dog and a garden. I used to have a decent garden, but these days I just plant a row or two of lettuce along the back. It's too much for me otherwise. Like that road out there. You're traveling just fine and then it turns on you. All those years I was going along, doing what I did and happy too, mind you. Then the road took its turns. Bad knees, lost friends, newfangled phones. Things slow you down, they take you someplace else."

She shrugs. "Every year I cut back on something. Weeding the garden, cooking a turkey, decorating a tree. It's funny how you love doing things until you don't. Just like that. No more stuffed turkey. I didn't expect it. I thought I'd always love doing everything I used to love doing. Then along comes a day when you say nuts to half of it." She gives me a long look. "It happens, Floria. Come a day you'll find something you won't want to do anymore. More than one," she adds.

I'm thinking how I've just left an entire life because I didn't want to do it anymore, but I don't say that. Instead I say, "My grandmother used to tell me *don'ta grow old*."

"How long did she live?"

"Ninety-three," I say and Maeve laughs and shakes her head.

"Was she sickly?"

"She lived in her own house until the very end. Ate the same breakfast every morning at nine a.m., cleaned with a rag tied over her broom, kept a pansy bed that was the talk of the neighborhood."

Maeve considers. "And what was it she ate for breakfast every morning?"

"One soft boiled egg, cooked three minutes, one slice of homemade bread toasted and buttered, and a half grapefruit, pink if in season."

"You see? There's always a reason people live long lives. My kids think I'm still around because I forget how old I am." She tips her chin toward the boat tied to her dock. "That's my rowboat. It's a pretty thing, isn't it?"

"It is. Maybe at some point I'll put in a dock too."

"But you go ahead and use my boat anytime you want. It came with the place and my son Joe, he's my youngest, he painted it that bright red. All the better to find me, I guess."

I tell her that the woman who lived in my cottage a long time ago left behind paintings, three of them—and that they all have a touch of that same red.

We watch a motorboat speed past our curve of the bay. Maeve says she always wanted to paint. "But you play the piano," I answer, thinking about that baby grand inside.

"I do. Nothing classical these days, but tunes. I can make me and Eddie happy with a few tunes, right, Eddie?" The dog is sound asleep now. "My mother was the real piano player. She grew up with education and privilege, you know, learned piano and a bit of drawing as well, the way cultured young women did at that time. But she married a locomotive engineer who moved her to a rough railroad town. She just never seemed to find her way. Then my father died of tuberculosis when I was nine and left her with three children and barely anything to live on, a widow's pension during the Depression. We had one lightbulb we moved from room to room, wherever we needed light." She catches herself going on and on. "I told you I talk too much."

But I'm interested. I want her to go on.

"My father's sister lived down the block and she took me under her wing. I was the oldest and I guess she wanted to teach me everything she thought my beleaguered mother could not—how to bake a cake, stitch a hem, set the table with the right silver. I was always torn between the two of them. I left home as soon as I could to become a nurse, met my husband, and seldom went back. I've never stopped regretting that I did not rescue my mother."

"You were young," I say. I see in her face that this is not reason enough for her abandonment. But she appreciates my effort. I see that too.

Our tea is done, the late afternoon lake getting populated. Maeve reaches for her straw hat sitting on the table and puts it on, tipping the brim forward to shade her eyes. That's how I leave her—on the deck, hat cocked, Eddie at her feet, and the vase of harebells close by.

# 5

## Chilled

Late evening a thick darkness descends and the rain begins, not gradually, but as though the sky has ripped wide open. The sound on my roof is deafening, the wind slams my porch door back and forth, and, thrilled by this, I light candles on my mantel. Then I see. One of the paintings has been knocked askew, the one with the tiny red house on a cliff. It's not just a hair off-kilter. It's tipped nearly sideways and I did not do this. I did not bump into the wall. I don't think I even came close to that wall of paintings. I turn to look in all directions, out onto the porch, even into the fireplace. Then I fix the painting.

I put on another opera, this time *The Marriage of Figaro*, nothing tragic, and sit facing the room, keeping guard. It's not that I expect a ghost to appear, but things happen. I know things happen. A radio goes on for no reason. A perfectly sturdy lamp falls to the floor. Images of loved ones appear near the bed, suspended soundlessly and refusing to leave. I know these things happen, they just have never happened to me.

Not that I don't appreciate a good mystery—disappearances unsolved, crazed wretches stowed away, trains winding through wilderness and always wilderness and overgrown woods, rickety bridges, unsavory strangers, crows at the window or door, fires raging and storms, like this one tonight. I love a good mystery. But this is my cottage, after all.

I turn up the volume on Mozart and gradually fall asleep, still in the armchair. When I awaken, it is nearly three in the morning, the candles have burned low, and the rain has slowed to a patter. I jerk my head toward the paintings and there they are, all in a row and level, just as I left them when I dozed off hours before. I build a fire and wrap myself in the wool plaid shirt I inherited from my husband. At one time it carried his scent, but now it carries only my own, along with the musty smell of clothing that has seen better days.

When he died, we were both in our thirties. We had been introduced by well-meaning friends locked in a lousy marriage who preferred gathering people around them rather than face the fact of their mutual dissatisfaction, and we married not even a year later. We liked each other immediately. At the time we married, he was teaching social studies in a city high school and beginning his doctorate to become a principal. A prince-of-a-pal, as he'd say.

But that never happened. What happened was that he chugged along in graduate school and taught tenth graders and bowled once a week in a league for high school teachers, and I traveled for my work as a researcher, and we remained a couple who liked one another and loved one another while living somewhat separate lives. When he and two of his teaching colleagues decided to visit South Africa—I no longer remember what they headed out to see—I did not go along. I had a project in Tuscaloosa, Alabama. I drove him to the airport and watched him walk through the double doors because it's important to get a last look before someone you love boards a plane.

He called me when they arrived. The next day they were going to drive from here to there, wherever it was, all of them excited to begin this adventure of a lifetime. Wish you were here, he said, and I remember telling him I wished I were there too rather than in Tuscaloosa and we laughed, it being so obvious. I didn't hear from him that day of touring and then on his second day there, the little rental car they were driving was hit head-on by a truck along a mountainous stretch of roadway. The truck driver was not expecting to see any cars, he traveled it often, had never had an accident before. That was the story I was told.

We'd been married six years. He's now been gone twice that long.

His mother was something of a spook, he thought, though

she died before I came along in his life so I cannot voice an opinion. Still, like I said before, we both tended to believe that forces moved about between this world and the next, that the old owner of a well-tended duplex might return to see what I was doing with her shelf paper. His mother had visitors all her life; her parents could barely stay on the other side according to family lore, haunting their daughter mercilessly, moving things, tilting and spilling and breathing in cold breaths all around her.

My husband's ancestors had come from Mexico in the early 1880s toward the end of the California Gold Rush, bringing with them a deep desire to live the good life and an equally deep faith in God, the Catholic Church, and the undeniable hereafter. His mother told him there were good spirits and bad, and that he must be on alert to know the difference.

When she died, she assumed the role of a good spirit, arriving in dreams with wise words for him and even an occasional joke, which he would relate to me later. Once on a night much like this one, with thunder rumbling and rain raging, I asked him to explain what his mother had meant about good spirits and bad. He shrugged it off. Good people become good spirits and bad people become bad spirits.

Nobody is all good or bad, I remember arguing. Of course, of course, he'd said. But you know what I mean. Sometimes darker energies prevail. He didn't think any of his spirit-based experiences were on the dark side, however. Nothing in his life had ever felt dark, I think, and now I'll never know.

He liked hearing from his mother after her death. Much more than she herself had liked hearing from her own tormenting parents with their disruptive afterlife manners. He said his mother would talk back to them all the time, urging them to go away, griping and fussing over their pranks.

Because I was young and open, I believed everything he said. And then later I had friends who reported visits by deceased parents or weird instances like the radio volume changing, the dial moved to a different station, that kind of thing, odd but harmless occurrences. Even friends who were not sure about

God seemed to be sure about spirits in some manner or another.

The escape artist Houdini apparently said if there was a way to return, he would do it, much as he bobbed back up from the deeps when he had been tossed overboard in a weighted trunk tied a hundred times with iron gables or some such. But we've never heard from Houdini. And I've never heard from my husband. Now it is so long ago, I have stopped any wondering I once had. If he'd wanted to swing by and say hello, he would have done it by now.

And considering all these things, I admit I'm sorry he has not.

# 6

## If I Loved You Wednesday

There were other men in my life, more like strangers on a train than lovers at the station.

Except for my marriage, I haven't ever shown the stamina to hold steady. My life has been unsettled in general since I left my family home. For a two-year stretch in my early twenties, I moved seven times. I had a small bookcase that held several boxes of my favorite books which I toted everywhere I lived. I had a typewriter because that was the era of typewriters. I had a hot pink alarm clock radio and a decoupage wall hanging that said *Bloom Where You Are Planted.* Which I more or less did. With my few possessions, I created a home with each move. The tortoise toting its shell.

In my early adult years, I found relationships to be something like excursions. I was there to see what I could see and learn what I could learn. Sometimes I had fun and sometimes not, but I never thought I'd stay. That went on for over a decade. The night I met my husband I was exhausted and frazzled. I had started a difficult work project that week and was grappling with news that my grandmother had had a stroke. I felt tired, ready to sit across the table from this man and exchange stories for a very long time.

All the years since his death, I seem to want neither adventure nor a long conversation, preferring quiet dinners that end definitively. I look back with fascination at my younger self. I look back wistfully at my married self. Now I am this self with the remnants of last night's raging fire in my stone fireplace and a lake beyond the door.

When I go outside to pick up twigs and branches blown off my trees in the storm, I see a tall redheaded man striding across Maeve's yard with Eddie at his heels. "Yo, you the new neighbor?"

He's come to tell me that his mother needs my phone number so she doesn't have to navigate the yard every time she wants to talk. He's not the youngest son, Joe, who painted her boat, but another son, Jimmy, who is named after his father and comes out to visit Maeve every Saturday.

"It's Saturday, is it?" I have been in my cottage for a full week.

"Lose track of time out in the sticks, do you?" He's a happy man, I see that. "My mother loves to make phone calls. It's the easiest thing to do. We all hear from her nearly every day and the older kids hear from her, too, which they love because Grandma listens when nobody else will. Now she wants to call you too." Beware, he adds.

"I haven't even turned my phone on since I moved here. Part of my plan to disappear," I say, which I deliver as a joke so he doesn't have to believe it. Still, I tell him my number. "But let your mom know I might not answer."

"She'll keep calling until you do."

"It's too bad she can't send Eddie over with messages, isn't it?" I look into the intelligent eyes of Maeve's dog.

"Mother wants to know if you'd like to join us all for dinner tomorrow noon. Sunday picnic sort of thing." He flashes a fake smile. "The Murphy clan."

"I'll see."

"Listen, don't worry. Wander over if you're in the mood. Or not." He repeats my phone number, calls to Eddie, and waves himself back through the bushes.

My phone is in a kitchen drawer. Every night I plug it in and every morning I stick it back in the drawer. It's a new number that so far nobody knows except my brother, who lives in another state and will seldom call anyway. I have kept all the collected contacts of my years in case I want to reach out to them. But they cannot call me. And if it matters to any of them now, it will not over time. They may care about me, may even be wondering or hurt by my abrupt and undisclosed departure, but this will soon be absorbed into their busy lives.

Stars die out and fall away while the universe barely gives notice. That's what I'm saying. Not that I don't treasure people. I already treasure my neighbor and her gentlemanly dog. And not that I am nonchalant. But I have become a realist over the years and my realistic view is that all those I have left behind will muddle along just fine without me and my phone number. Nonetheless, for Maeve's sake, I take the phone from the kitchen drawer and set it on top of my cookbooks.

She calls immediately. "I'm so happy to hear your voice. Jimmy says I'm not to trouble you, but I did want to test your number to make sure it works when I need it. You know my knees are not the best to go hobbling over for every little thing."

"You're welcome to reach out whenever, Maeve."

"And I hope we'll see you tomorrow so you can meet my family. We always have good food, you know. We do love our food."

"I'm a bit introverted for big gatherings. Don't feel bad if I don't show, okay?"

"Well, maybe for a minute or two? You think it over."

I say that I will and she goes on to ask how I survived the storm. "You can't claim a lake house until you've lived through a storm," she says.

I tell her about the twigs I've stacked out back for kindling and she says I'm to let her know if I need one of her boys to chop wood for me or anything, they'll be happy to do anything. "See you tomorrow," she says and disconnects so hurriedly I don't have time to answer. Just click and gone, like my grandfather used to do. Hello, goodbye, done.

I see how Maeve wants to include me in her life.

I'm someone new to her, another territory to know, and who doesn't want that now and then?

To fall in love a bit now and then?

# 7

## Such A Beautiful Lake

Saturday night passes without incident and the morning sky is perfection. Not a cloud, the blue high and unending. Behind my small house is a shack filled with storage boxes, tins, some appliances and gardening tools, all rusted, and a push mower, its paint long gone. The last time I mowed I was a child egging my dad to let me help him. All the years since, decades really, others have done this for me. Landlords, my husband, hired help. This mower I've inherited is stiff and difficult, so I make myself presentable and drive into town to the hardware store.

It's early. The one man working must be close to seven feet tall, slightly hunched in that way of very tall people, and sipping coffee in a Styrofoam cup. "What can I do you for?" he says without getting up off his stool. When I explain my difficulty with the mower he says he hasn't talked to anyone about a push mower in years.

I found it in my shed, I tell him. "I bought an old cottage on the bay."

"Oh sure," he says. "The Hale place, heard it got sold. Been there forever. I used to deliver to the Hales when I was a kid. So you bought the place, did you? You know John Hale was a legend around here years ago, ran steamboats back when, kind of a technology junkie. In his time, of course. Not our kind of tech junkie. But cars and boats, later radio and television. He had a whole workshop set up in that little place. Quite a guy. Smart. Quite a legend." He gazes past me out the front window of the store. "Course that was a long time ago. John died when I was in high school and his wife right before him. She was something too."

"A painter," I say.

"Well maybe, but she sure had a green thumb. Seemed to know everything about flowers and odd vegetables. Harvested seeds that went back centuries, things like that. We all thought the family would tear the house down and start over when John and Franny were gone, but they left it there, came and went once in a while, I guess, but it's been pretty empty for a long time. I mean, Franny and John died back in the seventies. Stayed in that place until the end. You going to fix it up much? I know contractors who can work on an old place like that."

"I think I'm just going to paint. And I probably need a couple of new screens. But I'm not looking for big changes. Or any changes. A dock," I say. "I'd like a dock."

He looks relieved. He delivered there as a kid and now he's middle-aged. He's seen too much change like everyone has seen too much change and now here I am saying I just want to add a dock. "I'm Harold," he says, offering a hand. I tell him I'm Floria, which is good enough for now. Then I buy primer, white outdoor paint, rollers, brushes, everything I need for my windows and trim, along with some type of oil for the mower. He tells me if that doesn't work to bring it in and he'll sharpen those blades for me. He also says he'll send someone on Monday to talk to me about a dock.

As he's helping load things into my car, he welcomes me to the community. "It's quite a lake here," he says. "Maybe a bit busy these days, but you stick to your bay there and let me know when you need anything."

So now I know a Harold.

And I know the names of the couple who owned my cottage.

Barely an hour later I look up from my cranky mower to see Maeve's son Jimmy making his way toward me. "Chicken's on the grill," he announces from halfway across my yard.

I want to finish my mowing and begin on my window trim. I have projects and a plan for this day, this cloudless, gorgeous day. Yet here I am, following Jimmy over to Maeve's where there are so many people, I know I will never keep them straight. They have a look, this Murphy family, and one jolly, intelligent face blurs to the next, children and adults. Only Eddie is distinct, and because I am an outsider, the dog comes to my feet and stays there. Maeve, too, is distinct and very pleased that I showed up. She tells me all her children's names, though two are not present today, one in Iowa for some reason and the other on her way to a banking conference in New York. The grandchildren are polite and busy, back and forth to the lake, back and forth to the table for more food or lemonade, their parents in familiar conversations that started decades ago and continue each time they are together.

"None of them even know I'm here," Maeve whispers to me. "Never listen when I talk." Then she laughs because she loves them so, but it does seem to be true.

Every person greets me with warmth, they are that kind of family, and a few talk briefly about my cottage, glad to have me next door, company for Mother. They ask who I am, where I lived before, what I do for work and I answer without answering. *Such a beautiful lake*, is my default. I say it again and again. I came to be by the lake. I've moved from a place that had no lake. I've paused my work to enjoy the lake. It makes perfect sense and, as Maeve says, they're not really listening anyway.

I've claimed a chair on Maeve's deck facing out at this beautiful lake, which today is at its most stunning, and I observe, which is my bent, and sip a beer, smiling all the while. When I sense it is fine to leave, I hug Maeve Murphy and thank her for including me.

"I'm going to put in a dock," I tell her and she nods as if it had been her idea in the first place.

Maybe it had been her idea.

I can't seem to recall.

# 8

## Starshine

I hear the Murphys all the while I finish mowing, then the crescendo of their farewells, car doors slamming, and the engines, a honk or two. I imagine Maeve now sitting in her recliner by the open window dozing for hours.

I am so satisfied with my lawn. I've gone end to end, from the edge of my small beach and my neighbors' foliage to my drive out back. Painting my windows is next. I work for hours and as I do, I absorb what surrounds me: motorboats on the lake, layers of laughter across the water, a medley of bird songs I do not recognize. A wind picks up, branches rustle. A truck or two passes on the road above and moment by moment, I have scraped and primed the front porch windows of my cottage until it is after nine and the lake has gone quiet. My work held me for so long that I did not feel time move and now the day is almost over.

No other part of the week shifts like Sunday evenings. Whoever all these people are here, whatever they do with their lives, they are now at the end of their weekend. Boats anchored, sandy, sunburnt children put to bed, leftovers wrapped for another day. With the last fragment of light, I hear an owl claiming the hours that belong to owls and the skittering creatures they swoop down to pursue. I am beginning to imagine what might be here. Beginning to see the outside trim fully painted, a dock installed, the beach cleared, those heirloom roses opening along my outer walls.

Maeve said the bushes between us are raspberries. They'll yield fruit soon. By mid-July the lake will be nearly as warm as a bath. Chives grow wild on the hill she told me as her family buzzed around us this morning. Good times, she implied. No end to them. I retell these things now. How it will be.

Without thinking I remove Fanny Hale's painting of the open sea to study her strokes more closely and to evaluate the framing. It's all well done, the frame heavy and nicely molded. I turn to the back and see a note glued there, yellowed by more than a century: *My Atlantic Home, New York, 1903. Frances Kay Lowen.* The words are printed in a confident script such that I see her, young Franny on shore, coming to paint the wild world of the sea, the boat on the horizon sailing away from her, and her watching it sail. Before long she would leave New York and travel inland, find a husband and this cottage on this lake and stay here for the rest of her life. Her hair is brown, her face shaped like a heart. She's grown up in a family that has the wealth to buy her paints and to frame her work in dark and lustrous frames, a cultured young woman like Maeve Murphy's mother. That is what I see.

I turn over the painting of the house on the cliff, but nothing is written there. The last, a vast beach with a woman walking in her red dress, has this in pencil, barely discernible: *Returning soon, you'll see. Love Franny.*

I situate all three paintings as they were, those darkening skies and touches of red. Does everyone think they will return? Surely my husband believed he would. My mother falling asleep the day of her death thought she was merely taking a late afternoon nap, so badly needed after all the day's effort. Houdini promised to return, more or less. And Franny. *You'll see.*

A cool June breeze comes in at all my windows, nothing uneasy or beckoning or otherworldly. Just lovely cool air. I have something to eat, take a long bath. On my way to bed I see that not one of the paintings is straight on the wall. I must have been careless in my placement. My evening glass of wine went to my head perhaps.

I adjust them with care and run my hands over the old frames. The moon is nearly full, throwing light across the room. I see so well even though the hour is late—all paintings aligned, the old table I've had for years steady next to my soft chairs near the fireplace. The tiny wallpaper roses appear to dance in the strange light and that is all there is.

Honestly, that is all.

# 9

## A You Or A Me

I awaken restless. Maeve has left a message to tell me her children found me so lovely, *thank heaven, Mother, you finally have a nice neighbor.* She is off to a doctor's appointment and lunch and if I call her back, please do not leave voicemail as she doesn't hear them that easily these days. By the time I am done listening to Maeve, a dirt-streaked van is coming down the drive, crushing pebbles as it descends to park alongside my door.

The man that Harold sent lopes out of his vehicle, untangles his arms and legs and knocks on the door. I see him look around as he waits for me to answer, his brown hair long and pulled into a ponytail. He has a beard, a bit shaggy, and his shirt hangs loose.

"You've got white pine," he says first thing. "You don't see so many of those here anymore."

"Why is that?" I know nothing of such things.

"All the usual reasons," he answers and scans my backwoods again. He is Bo Linney, he tells me, and follows me to the water, birds chattering on and on as they do in the mornings, and we talk about the dock, placement and size, the possibilities of decking. Wood, of course, I say, just an old-fashioned wooden dock. Wood requires upkeep, he explains. Plastic is pretty low maintenance, aluminum the easiest of all and the coolest, he adds, because it reflects the sun rather than absorbing it.

I own a cottage more than a century old that leans just slightly on the southerly slope of the land. My refrigerator seems to me only one generation past the ice box and I feel fortunate to have indoor plumbing and a washing machine. I can't picture a plastic or aluminum dock here. That's what I say.

"It's the future though." His eyebrows lift and his shoulders as well. Then he takes a small notebook out of his back pocket, retrieves the pencil from behind his ear, and scribbles my order—the cedar dock, the approximate length. He doesn't ask my name. He doesn't say what a charming cottage I have. He does continue to take in the trees all around us, however, as if he knows them personally and is pleased to see them again.

"I'll come by later today or tomorrow with an estimate for you. Probably start in a week, maybe sooner."

I ask if he's been doing this work for a while.

"A while," he says like it is a joke with himself. "I've done lots of things for a while." He puts his notebook back in his pocket and turns to leave.

"What kinds of things?"

"I used to mine uranium. Then I worked tugboats in the Gulf of Mexico. Taught high school once for a year. If it weren't for parents, I'd probably be teaching still." He shrugs, not an apology, but something close.

I say that my husband was a high school teacher. That he wanted to be a principal someday. I don't know why I bring this up really, it's so far in the past.

"What's he do now?" Bo Linney asks.

When I tell him my husband died in a car crash on a South African switchback, he says he's sorry and looks straight at me. He doesn't dodge the comment as so many people do, something I've learned over time. There are those willing to meet loss head-on and those who prefer to sidestep its very mention.

"Thing is," this man Bo says, "it's a big world. Good to have a few adventures, right?" Then he gets into his van that is rusted on all fenders. I find myself calling thank you as he drives away, but I don't think he hears me.

It's barely midday. After finishing some cleanup in the cottage, I make my way to Maeve's dock, take a good look at how it's constructed, the worn wooden planks that jut much farther into the lake than mine will. I untie her red rowboat and push away. There is a bit more wind than I expected, but I move at a steady pace, bobbing along with the increasing waves. Just far enough out, I pull in the oars and lean back, close my eyes and drift. Above me clouds travel, covering the sun then blowing on by again, humongous, billowing cumulus clouds.

When I was a girl, we followed clouds like these. Lying flat on the grass, we'd call out the shapes we saw: it's a rabbit, an elephant, your mother's hairdo. This was a game, as much as anything. Some of us had bikes and some had roller skates, but the world itself, life itself, was really what we had. We might sit for an hour trying to close one eyelid at a time or lift one eyebrow without lifting the other. We played war, house, and school. We played visiting. And church, using Saltines for communion. Anywhere was anything. A tree would be a mountain and we would climb that mountain to see for miles, watch ships sailing in from the yard next door.

The wind is becoming fierce now, gusting in from the south, which might mean warmer weather on its way, I don't know. Out here on the lake there seems to be much I don't know. White pines, lawn mowers, and the names of little blue flowers growing on my hill. I have been a professional researcher since I graduated from college. My clients pose questions they want answered and I set about getting them answers. Nobody expects me to know the answer at the start.

And what is knowing anyway? Shelves of books full of facts and teachers full of facts at their podiums and well-educated friends full of facts. Names of creatures, symptoms of disease, rules of composition, who wrote what, built what, said what, went where. And none of these the underset. None of these the murmur that tells you when tempers will shift, what darkness means, if this time is the right time.

Suddenly the lake is becoming dangerous and the wind pitches me about too vigorously. I row against the waves and just as I pull alongside Maeve's dock, the rain comes, neither light nor gentle, such that I am soaking wet before I have even tied the rowboat in place. I hurry into the cottage to close my windows against the torrent, which seems to angle in from every direction.

I build a fire and sit for a time watching, so lulled by the snap in the old logs and the flaming color that I do not notice the afternoon passing and day coming to its end. The fire is near embers, and the face before me barely there. Her chin is not quite as I pictured, more round than heart-shaped, but just as youthful, the eyes wide and far apart. A sign of beauty, my mother would say.

I know it is Franny Hale.

# 10

## Deep Into Darkness Peering

"Franny?" I hear myself ask. "Can I do something for you?"

She gives no answer, no signal.

"Is it you?"

This is what I say to the wafting illusion in my cottage. And though I sense that she has something to convey to me, I hear nothing and see nothing that might indicate her purpose.

Then the room is empty again.

"Franny?"

I try this several times, turn to assess all corners of the cottage until it is doubtless I am alone. And suddenly, this short night just days past the summer solstice feels long and dark. I add logs to the fire and, for the second time since I moved here, spend the entire night in the more kindly of my two chairs, monitoring the fire and my heartbeat and waiting for the early glimpse of dawn. Franny Hale is a good spirit, I assure myself. And technically, this home on the lake was hers for over a century—seventy years of her life and seemingly decades after. Nobody else settled in as I am doing, swept floors and arranged furniture, shelved books and put wildflower bouquets on the mantel. What did Harold over at the hardware store say? Family came and went. They didn't put historic dinnerware in the cupboard and paint the window trim.

The last woman who did those things was Franny Hale.

Perhaps I should worry. Perhaps Franny Hale has no intention of letting me live in what was once hers. And how will I know? Researchers are trained to dig, to not accept what appears to be or might be, but to keep on, find another source, investigate possibilities just in case they lead to a better answer.

So how to uncover the meaning of Franny Hale in my midst? What is there to investigate with things like this, a face in the dull light of evening, artwork tipped askew? What would a woman like Franny want after all these years of absence? If, in fact, she has been absent. Such are the things I wonder as the hours of night pass.

An owl in these woods hoots during the day. I never see it, but I can point to the tree where it perches and speaks. This early morning the owl is part of a chatter on all sides of the cottage, up in the birches and out on the lake. The sky is still moody, as it was late yesterday, but there is light now.

And that is what I need.

# 11

## Neither Here Nor There

I come into the hardware store to find Harold ringing up an ancient-looking fellow ranting about the state of this small lakeside town. "I'm running for mayor next year, Harold, that's what I'm doing. Somebody's got to bring some sense to things around here." He grabs his weed killer off the counter and tells me to vote for Mel Lish next ballot. "You won't be sorry," he says.

"Bo been out to see you?" Harold pops a stick of gum into his mouth. "You know I don't refer him to some of these types around here, good as he is, the guy just ticks them off. Doesn't kowtow, if you catch my drift."

I say that Bo seems perfect for the job, I'm sure he'll do well by me. But I have something else on my mind. "Harold is there any more you can tell me about Franny Hale and her husband? Anything really. Old gossip or about their kids or how they died?"

Harold's trying. "Let me think. So she died first, I remember that."

"In the cottage? Did she die in the cottage?"

"Out in the yard there. My mom told me because I liked those two, couple of characters, I thought, projects going all the time, even at their age." He's back more than half a lifetime and I see that for him, it's a good place to be, a known world. "Right, so Franny died putting her garden to rest for the season. Maybe late September. Yup, that was the story. John found her out there, happy to the end. Then John, let me think, something similar a few months later. I mean they didn't linger. It just happened, the way we all want to go in the end."

"How about kids? Did you know their kids?"

"They had a couple of boys, kind of late I think, and both went off to war. John too, he'd been in the war to end all wars, told me a story now and then, and how Franny was a wreck when he went off. And the whole time her boys were overseas too. Anyway, after the war, the kids settled elsewhere. Never saw either of them personally."

"So how old do you think the Hales were when they moved into my cottage?"

"Well, I was a sophomore in high school when Franny Hale died. It was the year I was doing deliveries for a family grocery, that's why I remember. Anyway, it would have been 1975, and she was in her late eighties. So they were pretty young when they moved in." He gives me a hard stare. "You uncover some artifact or something?"

I tell him three paintings were left behind, but otherwise no. No artifacts.

"Except that lawn mower." Harold laughs. "You got to call that an artifact, don't you think? Dig around some more in that shack of theirs, who knows what you'll find." He laughs again.

I'm home in less than ten minutes, anxious to go back inside my shed. It's a mash-up of life's leftovers, the boxes nearly disintegrated, the few tools rusted like the lawn mower. There's a stack of radios and radio parts, deteriorated rakes, a halfway decent shovel and a wrecked broom. I see a broken fan in one corner, heavy metal tins labeled screws, nails, files, and the like, and I go through one after another but uncover nothing unusual. Nothing revealing. The tins themselves are heavy and substantial though, and I choose two of them to use for storage in the cottage.

I find magazines too damaged for rescue and newspapers the same, but old papers are so tempting to the researcher in me that I try to unfold them anyway, disappointed as one after another falls apart in my hands. I find broken Christmas tree decorations, dried oil paints, and petrified artist's brushes. There is one box of seed catalogs from the 1930s, covered in plastic for some reason, and all these catalogs remain in pristine condition. Some names I recognize like Burpee, others—WW Barnard Company Seedsmen and R. Dunning—speak of another time. They're beautiful, the illustrations and detail, and so I haul them all into the cottage to browse through later.

When I step outside to clean up the military tins, I see that Bo Linney has arrived. "Nice old ammo boxes," he says climbing out and handing me his estimate for the dock.

"Is that what they are? I found them in the shed."

"Looking for anything specific?"

"Just piecing together the past."

"Well, it's an old place. If you're okay with the bid, I'll start on Friday." I glance at the estimate, smudged by his fingers and folded unevenly. I tell him it looks good, but he does not leave.

"That's a great shed you've got. I love places full of junk, kind of shows how people live. Lots of houses here, there's no disorder, no hanging on to useless things for the hell of it. Everything's in rows or stuffed away somewhere. I don't know. You're lucky to have all this."

That's all he says. Then he hops in his van and rattles up to the road. In his wake the air seems very still. I stare at the old shed, trying to imagine what it looked like when John and Franny Hale first built it here, the hardware on the door shiny, the floor level for some years before it started to sink into the hill. Maybe their boys hid in the shed when they didn't want to come to dinner or played cops and robbers around the shed the way boys want to play cops and robbers. Maybe the Hale boys were like that.

I finish cleaning the metal tins and take them inside, shocked to find that the stack of seed catalogs I left on the table is now scattered all over the floor, as if shoved off in one aggressive swipe. I glance around like I always do, but of course there is no one in the cottage, not even the illusion of Franny Hale.

I pick the catalogs up off the floor, sorting them by year, and then begin to page through them one by one, trying not to think about what force removed them from my table. They are much more interesting and elaborate than modern seed catalogs, the descriptions flamboyant, the graphics lively and artistic and probably worth something if I cared to sell them online or at auction. The cover drawings tend to feature one or two pieces of produce, like a giant pumpkin, ruby beets, berries still on the vine. The stems curve, the colors pop, and I see that the seeds of that time are not all the same as what we buy and plant now, that there are phases and fashions of vegetables, of all things.

I bring out a bottle of wine, put together a fast sandwich and keep going. I'm in the fourth or fifth catalog when I come upon a charcoal sketch of a young man, done on heavy paper that has been protected between the pages. The drawing is not amateurish, but subtle and evocative, the face of someone you'd like to know. He's looking straight at me now, eyes alight with humor and something else. Affection, perhaps. The subject liked his sketcher. When I turn the paper to the back, it is labeled *Charles M. 1918.*

My breath catches on this bit of information. It was during the war, the war John Hale later told stories about and, clearly, Franny drew the image. I move on to the next seed catalog and the next. I go through the entire stack of close to forty catalogs ranging from the early 1920s through the 1930s, one just as beautiful as the one before. I find several more drawings that I take to be the work of Franny Hale, her style consistently light, almost impressionistic, expert and engaging.

Of the seven sketches, three are of Charles, but only the first has been labeled with his name. The second of him says *Saturday Night*, a full body sketch, the man leaning against a chair which is not fully delineated, his look intense and serious. The last, labeled *Leaving* is a profile of Charles, hair mussed, the chin angled forward, as though the man is already on his way to another destination. Neither has a date. The remaining four sketches are of plants—the branch of a raspberry bush, a single rose stem, grapes on the vine, and a bouquet of wildflowers. All in charcoal. Without color.

At this moment, I am as much in Franny Hale's world of a

century ago as I am in my own. I see that whatever the loves of her life, she refuses to let them go.

She wants me to know that.

# 12

## What Chaos May Occur

My grandmother once said to me, "You no buy trouble. Even if you no buy, you get." A new morning and still agitated, I am mulling these words. I've come to this cottage on an uncorked whim, not risking much and asking even less. I would not say I've bought trouble. I would not say I've bought anything more than a couple of rooms in the middle of nowhere.

Without making coffee or toast or even drinking a glass of water, I put on my painting clothes and go outside to work on my windows. I finish the porch screens on the south side of the house and then I keep going to the back of the house. The sun is faint, as though it traveled farther away in the past twenty-four hours, barely able to signal its existence. I hear my neighbors with the long dock who are somewhere high above ground today, on a balcony or deck. There are many of them, their voices high and low, overlapping, punctuated by short bursts of laughter. Very normal and agreeable.

They would not think a spirit moved about right next door to them. They would never believe such a thing. They probably would not quite believe the likes of me either, abandoning a life for this narrow strip of property that must appear an aberration to them. My cottage more a boathouse than a house.

By the time I realize that I am famished, I have scraped both back windows and the door and have not yet worked myself into a calm state of mind. Going inside to make a sandwich, I remain restless. I put two pieces of bread in the oven to make toast and as I wait for them to brown, I glance around the main room of the cottage where, once again, every single painting by Franny Hale is crooked on the wall. I fix the paintings, slap cheese and lettuce into my sandwich, and eat it standing up in the middle of the room.

This is when I hear my mother admonishing me for isolating myself such that I have nobody to turn to at a time like this. Or at any other time of trouble, which—as my grandmother warned—is always bound to come. Order in the universe being only partial, after all. Things holding in place only more or less, planets orbiting suns and moons hanging on to their favorite planets. But also clumps of matter plunging and shooting about. One never knows what chaos may ensue. Life is a continuous fixer-upper really. This I tell myself.

I gulp half a beer and take the rest outside where I start up my work again. At least here, I am in charge. I'm good with a brush and the white paint glistens like the hour after rain. When I have finished, I go down to the shore and start yanking weeds, this so therapeutic I think essays should be written on it. I wade into the water and pull and toss and pull and toss, breathing heavily like a wild beast hunting for buried food. And then, without thinking about it, I take off my baggy shirt and start to swim through the disgusting weeds, flapping past them, ignoring the weird tickle against my skin as I move outward toward cleaner water.

I am a very bad swimmer. The first time my husband saw me in action he asked in wonder how I had ever managed to pass high school swimming. "The teacher gave up and put me in my own lane," I told him, and when he asked why, I said, "So she didn't have to think about me." In fact, I took lessons multiple times in my life to be the very bad swimmer that I am. As a result, I know the better parts of many strokes. If my forward flapping gives way, I roll over and do something of a backward thing and part of a butterfly thing. And that is what I do now to overcome Franny Hale's unrelenting presence, I cut through the water any way I can until I am free of the snaring weeds and heading straight for Maeve Murphy's dock. I don't see Maeve outside, haven't seen her in days, but that doesn't matter. Her dock feels familiar and safe.

The sun remains far away and I bask in its light. Once relaxed, I realize I am also exhausted. I stagger back to my own beach, pick up my shirt and drag myself inside to take a bath, warm the soup, and drink some wine. That's when I see there is a voicemail on my phone. It is from Maeve's daughter asking me to call and, even listening to the message twice, I do not pick up any clues that might prepare me for whatever news the daughter has for me. I call back and she answers instantly, thanks me for reaching out. Then she tells me her mother fell the day before. "We don't think it's anything serious, but Mother wanted you to know. She'll be going back to her house tomorrow with nurses there to help until she can walk a bit on her own. You're welcome to visit any time. You know she loves your company."

I fumble with this news, say yes I will be here waiting for her return, and the call is quickly over. It's nice they let me know. Interesting that I have already and unwittingly made enough of a connection to be on the family's short list for bad news.

A slice of sun cuts across my front doorway. Every painting is still in place and the stacks of seed catalogs as well. I think I am alone. I came to be alone, imagined things that way. But here are Maeve Murphy and her children, Harold at the hardware store, Bo Linney, and Franny Hale. My mother and father giving advice, my grandmother staring back from her other world.

Truthfully, I am surrounded.

# 13

## Always A Rose

The cabbage roses have bloomed. When I hear a car in Maeve's drive, I snip enough stems for two bouquets. I do not spend the time to arrange them but set one on my mantel and take the other with me. I find her at her dining table, a walker by her side, exhaustion in all her features. "I did not anticipate this, Floria," she says as I come in with my roses. She shrugs unhappily, tosses her head toward the woman at the kitchen sink putting together tea, pills, and what have you. Maeve rolls her eyes like a teenager told to be home by ten. "My nurse," she declares.

"Well, that's okay, Maeve. She'll just help out." I lower my voice. "It's still your home. You're still in charge."

"Am I?"

She then tells me what happened. She and her youngest son had gone to a garden center to look at shrubs for his yard. She was there to advise and they were conversing as they moved among the plants. But a wave of vertigo came over her and she lost her balance at a moment when Joe was too far ahead for her to grab onto his arm. She remembers saying his name as she started to go down, but he didn't hear her. Such an awful thing, that he couldn't hear her, and she had to keep falling alone onto the wet concrete, other shoppers around and nobody quick enough to prevent her from hitting the ground. "Every which way, Floria," she declares, surprised and angry that it should be so, that her legs would twist in odd positions and her arms flail so hopelessly. "I just couldn't stop my fall. I just could not. Imagine," she says, "down like an apple too ripe for the tree. And that was that."

"What exactly is wrong?" She has no bandages or cast on her body. No bruises that are visible. Nothing that would seem to warrant nurses around the clock.

"I can't walk. Well, barely. I can shuffle hanging on to this thing." She swats the walker beside her. "But I can't really stand up on my own or lower myself on my own. I didn't break anything, but I hurt things, they say. Knocked myself out of whack, I guess."

"So you'll heal soon enough and be on your own again." This seems a logical thing to say, not just wishful thinking.

"Maybe." She doesn't look at me.

"My cabbage roses are in bloom," I say and slide the haphazard bouquet in front of her, smile as she inhales deeply. She holds her breath for long seconds and exhales with her eyes closed.

"Thank you, dear. This is the best thing I've known in days. Are they a wild rose, do you think? Just kind of sprung up over time?"

I say I believe the long-time owner planted them decades ago, maybe even a century ago. "The woman was quite a gardener, I guess. Franny Hale was her name. She was known for her green thumb, rare cultivated seeds and the like."

"Franny Hale," she repeats the name. "Did she die over there?"

"I hear that she did. Out in her garden."

"That's nice. I'd like my last sight of this world to be of that lake out there."

"Maeve, have you ever seen anything odd at my place or sensed anything over the years before I moved here?"

"You mean when no one lived there?"

"Just wondering. Never mind." I realize this is not the conversation that Maeve needs right now and change the topic. I tell her I've got most of my windows primed, that things are looking good. And now the roses have bloomed as well.

Maeve settles back to drink her tea. "I don't even much like the kind of roses you buy in stores, most of them don't have a scent. But these, my-my. You've made my day, Floria. How could you know?" She carefully sets her cup on the table and in an instant she is asleep. The effort it took her to get into her house again and greet me, talk, and drink that cup of tea with her little pile of pills was more than enough for her. I pull my chair away quietly to leave and that's when I notice Eddie, lying under the table, his chin flat on his front feet and his eyes staring at the carpet.

When I whisper his name, he moves one ear.

# 14

## When Again This

My neighbors to the south have lights on their dock that illuminate my shoreline at night. It's a white, eerie glow reflecting off the water, and tonight I see two large birds join just above the lake's surface then rise together in a swirl of wings and energy, their span magnificent and unworldly. I do not know if they are owls or hawks, surely not gulls, and rising, they disappear into the darkness. After watching for some time, I pick up the book I left on the porch days ago and return inside. And there is Franny Hale, in front of the stone fireplace, her features blurred, her presence undeniable.

She is not thin air, it's important for me to make that clear. I can see her delicate face, wisps of what would be hair pulled back into a topknot of sorts, a classic, old-fashioned look. She wears a blouse, white even in transparency and she is unsettled, wavering, almost summoning.

I feel her disquiet and this is not all. Suddenly I, too, have a longing, not for one thing in particular, but for everything I've known—my family, my childhood, my husband and friends who have faded into time. I take a deep breath and when I do this, I am filled with the scent of the roses on my mantel. And it stays. Even when I exhale, I hold the scent of those rampant roses Franny Hale once planted all around the cottage she called home, roses she knew every year thereafter.

And then she is gone. I mean she is no longer before me. She doesn't turn and exit or make her departure. She just suddenly is not here.

I slide against the wall to the floor, clutching my knees tightly. Everything inside the cottage stays still, and it is a resting and relieved stillness, like my own breath now, rhythmic and comfortable again. Nothing in the room is changed and I am not changed. Something has happened to me, but I am not changed.

Only weeks ago I lived in a rented second-floor apartment with ceilings that soared fifteen feet above parquet floors, the windows paned and tall, very French I thought, and I had double doors out to a balcony where I would sit on summer mornings to drink my coffee. I was there for many years. Every spring I filled planters on that balcony, one of purple pansies that reminded me of my grandmother and one of orange nasturtiums that reminded me of my mother, and these flourished in the afternoon sun, the same sun that would pour into my living room and galley kitchen.

I moved there after my husband died, needing to distance myself from the house where we'd spent our short married life. I had friends in that other life, people who called to say hello and go for neighborhood walks, who came to dinner and invited me to see the opera, a play, or a baseball game. They were busy people or they appeared busy, determined to make life matter and do well and do some good too, that is also true. They were, to a person, interesting. But I was lonely anyway. I longed for another place and this is that place. All wisdom aside, I thought that coming to this cottage I would escape my own longing.

Now here is Franny Hale to say otherwise.

# 15

## To Talk Of Many Things

I must have finally fallen asleep deeply for I do not hear Bo Linney when he parks his van in my driveway and hauls the many pieces of my dock down to shore. I do not hear him until he begins drilling and by then it is midmorning. I dress and go outside to see how he is doing, wooden beams and poles now lined up on the lawn and two pilings installed deep in the water. He stops working when he notices me, grabs a battered lunch pail near him, and pulls out a thermos. He pours his coffee into the screw-top cup and says, "Nice day."

"It looks like quite an operation. You started early?"

"Always do. I like to be done working before three, get ahead of the traffic."

"You don't live nearby then?"

"Out of my league," he says and glances over to me. "Your place, maybe not. I could live in a place like this. But I've got a bungalow about thirty miles west. Small town with small houses, kids playing in the streets, dogs in every yard."

"I grew up in a town like that," I say. Then we're quiet. A couple of boats go past at the mouth of the bay, one towing a water-skier. I ask if Bo is a nickname for something.

"I made it up," he answers. "My real name is William Merrill, same as my dad. He was a banker, so it worked for him. But I started calling myself Bo when I was about five. Sounds good, don't you think? Bee Bop Bo." He downs his coffee and stands. "How about you? What do you call yourself?"

"Floria," I say.

"You made that up."

I say, "No, it's from the opera *Tosca.*"

"Shoot, I know that. But you made it up, too, didn't you?"

I say that I did and he says he knew it and goes back to work, not questioning why I would do such a thing. He's sure and methodical, his whole process of putting in my dock as much a dance as labor. There's a rhythm to it all and a pleasure in it as well. Watching him soothes me. He starts drilling again, making way for the dock's pilings, he tells me, apologizing for the noise.

But I choose to stay. It's odd for me not to be working. I have always worked, beginning when I was fourteen and the woman across the street hired me to babysit her toddler. I don't remember the baby, but I do remember the woman's frosted, back-combed hair and the expensive wools she wore, her printed Scandinavian sweaters with silver buttons. She gave me twenty-five cents for the entire stint, anywhere from one to three hours, and even then, I knew this was not right. But when she called, I went, because it was a job. Before I became a researcher, I put in time as a waitress in more than one restaurant, worked in a clothing store, filed vouchers in an office, tutored reading, and, very briefly, assisted a fire-baton twirler at a somewhat shady nightclub. I know work.

In my immigrant family, it meant survival—all the fixing, growing, making and making do, all the scrubbing and stitching and canning and cooking, the fishing and farming. That said, everyone in my family had their diversions. My father loved his sports, my mother her books. My grandfather played canasta for nickels and my grandmother never missed her afternoon soap operas. Me, here and now, I spend hours on end just watching the lake slap against the shore and recede. Weather moves through, sometimes visible for miles, the late-day darkness deepening and rolling forward. My reward for all the years of work.

At noon Bo breaks again. "You going to eat something?" He takes out a wrapped sandwich. "You can have half of this, just cheese and relish." But I say no, I'll get something soon.

"What did you teach back when?" I venture.

"Guess."

"Guess? Not something boring," I say. "Physics maybe?"

"Close, very close. I taught English."

"And that is close to physics?" He does not answer. "My husband taught history," I tell him. "He got into the stories. All tall tales, he would say. He liked teaching."

"It's good to like your work. Otherwise it's a long life, right? Every job I ever had there'd be the lifers complaining about this and that and this and that, and I'm listening to them thinking, 'Then why don't you do something else?' But it's the pension or it's the benefits or it's the lazy ass unwilling to take a risk. Pardon me. As soon as I don't like what I'm doing, I'm gone. Hence I cannot afford to live on this lake. Or take an Alaskan cruise, which has always sounded nice to me. But," he shrugs, "I am not unhappy and that's the sum of it." He crumples his sandwich bag into the lunch pail, snaps the lid shut.

He stands surveying my property. "This place of yours is quite a find."

"That's what the realtor said. A steal, she said. But it was on the market for a few months at least. I don't know why. She told me it's because people want more land to build larger houses. This wasn't even worth the tear-down, she said, the lot is so narrow. And the cottage is rough, you know old and never updated."

"You must have some good karma," he says and returns to his pilings.

Karma? I wonder about that. Is there such a thing? Or destiny, some underlying plan with blessings bestowed and benefits rendered? Or is there only happenstance? Only a bit of good luck that I saw the real estate listing for this cottage on a lake one hundred miles around and was pulled toward it blindly, running away with a few possessions on a cool morning in June.

I call out to Bo that I'm heading inside, but his drill overwhelms my words. I come through the screened porch with some hesitancy, find no disorder, feel no pulse of disquiet. All the windows are open to the late June air and any bit of clutter here is all my own.

# 16

## My Funny Valentine

Bo leaves at three as he said, stopping by the back door to say he'll return Monday morning. I stay at the door as he lumbers off, his engine straining to make it up the steep hill, then I cut a few more roses for Maeve and walk over to see how she is doing. I feel better in the orbit of others today, better avoiding the wanting which Franny has left to me. A nurse opens the door at Maeve's and wanders off without a word.

In one day, every book and paper has been removed or organized, the music closed on the piano, all signs of creative enterprise tucked away. I don't even see my jar of roses. "Floria, I am just crumbly here," Maeve says from her spot by the window. She is in a wheelchair now, her walker nowhere in sight. "Every hour I get worse."

I set the flowers on the table and pull a chair to sit near her. "Are you sleeping?" I ask. "Eating well, moving about at all?" I get answers that tell me less than the downward turn of her features. "I'm so sorry, Maeve."

"Well, I am too. What the devil even happened to me? Last weekend I was doddering about just fine, wasn't I, Eddie?" She stretches out a hand to him and he parks himself perfectly within her grasp. "All the family was here and I was fine. This way of being old does not interest me, Floria."

"You fell just days ago, Maeve. You'll improve. Keep resting, move around a bit. I know you'll improve."

"I see an end," she says so soundlessly I wonder if I heard her say it.

"What happened to your roses?"

"One of these women moved them by the bed. Which is

fine, I suppose. Well-meaning." Her tone says otherwise.

I tell her I've brought more and get up to set my second bouquet on the piano, its keys dusted and waiting. "Maeve, you want to play something for me?" I take hold of the wheelchair and roll her to the baby grand, pull the bench out of the way, and glide her in. Just this bit of activity gets Eddie's tail wagging and when Maeve does a scale, smooth and skilled, he murmurs. She opens a song book to "My Funny Valentine" and begins, her arthritic fingers defying pain, her focus all on the sweet music she is making.

When she comes to the last note of the song and I clap in response, she shakes her head, maybe surprised at herself, maybe something else. "My mother taught me that song. A child named Mitzi Green first sang it in a musical. How's that for memory? It's a very old song."

"But still current," I say, thinking I've heard recordings of it at one time or another, Chet Baker maybe or Frank Sinatra.

"You know, I didn't like learning piano from my mother because she played so well. Not that she got impatient, I wouldn't say that. But I never liked how I sounded in comparison. Oh, aren't we all so impossible?"

She begins playing again, this time "My Favorite Things" from *The Sound of Music.* I know enough of the words to jump in with her, leaning on the piano like a club singer, hitting barely half the notes. It's a grand moment. Then Maeve tells me she needs to lie down and to please ask the nurse cleaning the bedroom to come and help her. I do as she asks and slip away.

Clouds have gathered again in this wet month of June, a rumble far off and then another. I hurry home to shut windows before it rains. I don't think to look around for signs of Franny Hale, it's been hours since I've thought of her. Bo building my dock was so real, the noisy drilling of the lake floor, the wrapped pilings going into the ground, his battered thermos of coffee. Then Maeve struggling for herself, the heavy wheels of her chair, her head bowed in weariness, those songs filling that oddly ordered house.

But now, reaching to close the bathroom window, I hear something fall and I remember. This time it is just one painting, the one of the woman in the red dress, and it has fallen face down, which may or may not be intended. I say nothing. I hang the painting, and, as the rain begins to pelt my front porch screens, I stand at the door getting wet and watching the rain water drum against the lake's surface.

The notes of "My Funny Valentine" play out in my mind. It's a song of Franny's generation, I think, when she might have sung along to the radio her husband knew how to repair, might have hummed as she planted heirloom lettuces in her garden, might have had someone sing just for her. And then would she have sung this song in return? To John? To the man she sketched in 1918? I belt out the few lines I know and wait to see if she will respond.

But, of course, she does not.

# 17

## The Wind Is Passing By

I am not in charge. What music Franny Hale may love, when or if art will fly off the wall or Franny float through the room, disturb, or long for another time, I cannot determine. I live with a ghost. Maybe last week I thought this with curiosity and a bit of fear. Now I'd like to understand.

As the rain drives down on my shingled roof, I dig my laptop out of the drawer where I've stored it since I moved here and I search for information about Franny Hale's kind of returning. It's such a murky area, nothing I pull up is definitive or satisfying. It's all subliminal fact or mystical experience, one article says. I read that ghosts are not spirits, or not the same as spirits, because ghosts stay in one place whereas spirits wander, often aimlessly. Ghosts tend to remain because they don't want to leave, they like where they once were and are now. Entire books have been written to explore this thin line between what is here and what is there, this life and the next.

I grew up with people from old countries, where death was never casual, never a bit player. When it came, we paid attention, and it always came as it always comes, and we'd honor its largeness and permanence. We had smoky rooms back then where we gathered, men sitting in deep-cushioned chairs around the television set. Jackets removed and ties loosened, white shirts in contrast to dark pants and black polished shoes. Their hair was slicked, and even in the shadow of death, there was, in those rooms of men, a sensual vibrancy. The end of life pulling forth the verity of living, sweaty hunger beneath starched and buttoned shirts. My older cousins had that glint in their eyes, an awakening. I remember that.

The kitchen would be filled with steam, brightly printed aprons covering black dresses. And so much food—on platters and in bowls and little relish dishes meant for olives, black and green, pimento or no. Wine, mostly homemade, and highballs with cherries bobbing amidst the ice cubes. Everyone drank. Even children had something. A sip of Mogen David at least.

We told stories with enormous, gut-wrenching laughs. I remember it like a dream that does not end. Everyone there and the smoke enveloping us. Nothing like this airy place where I am now. And nothing that spoke of returning, of restless souls wandering back our way. I've kept my parents and grandparents close, as I've said, letting them boss me around now and then and guide me, their voices a comfort and constant in my life. Turn off the light on your way out the door. Rinse the dishes before the food goes hard. Pinch back the plants. Make your bed. But all this is something of memory, of hanging on to what I have known. It is not phantasmal.

My research describes ghosts who are menacing and reckless, throw things and intentionally make trouble. Like my husband's grandparents. I read of ghostly spiritual quests, the regathering at lands of slaughter, at scenes of tragedy, sites of wrongful deaths and murders. Residual energy, I read. Moments of time in confluence. Souls tangled together over centuries. None of this scientific. None of it definitive.

If I want to simply think my way through death and the afterlife I would say, as many people I know say, that the ground is hard where we will lie forever gone. There will be no reversal. So, if I am thinking my way through this, whatever I see and experience with Franny Hale must be some anomaly of my imagination. Is that it? My father shrugs. My grandmother tips her head to the side like she always did when she did not believe a word you were saying. My mother picks up another mystery book and pretends she doesn't hear me. That is what my ancestors tell me about returning.

It is late and the sound of the rain steady. I spread Franny's drawings across my old table, studying them as though they have something specific to say to me, as though this handsome man Charles will reveal the story of why she drew him, how they knew one another, what it meant. One light is on in my cottage, but it is some feet away from where I stand staring at Charles of 1918 and so he rests in evenfall and shadow.

I choose to think he was an old friend of Franny's from the East. He came here to see her one time before losing himself to the last days of the war. John was not at home, but Charles may not have known that. He does not look like the wolfish sort. He found Franny alone with her garden of unusual vegetation, her roses surrounding the cottage and her paintings hanging on its walls. Let me draw you, she would have said, because that would have been a way to hold him close for some minutes and keep him with her afterward. Maybe they weren't ever in love. Maybe he was her cousin, a brother, the treasured son of childhood neighbors. Maybe they'd sailed together when they were young, their hair blowing like crazy in the ocean winds. Maybe he asked her to paint the house high on the cliff with its red roof or the woman in red on the beach. Then he came to find her. Then he went away.

I arrange the three drawings of Charles on my table in the order I believe Franny did them—the affectionate stance first, the full portrait second, the leaving image last. Then I turn off the light. Outside the bedroom window I hear the screech of an owl alarmed by something in the rainy night. Or declaring its victory over some other poor creature. Or merely announcing to the darkness that it has found the owl of its dreams.

I am full of stories here.

# 18

## Who Keeps & Who Forgets?

I sleep through the break of dawn and the fog's slow burning, awaken forgetting it is Saturday or even that it is the month of June. I dream I am on a beach I've never known, watching a girl in a red dress walk alone as waves break over her bare feet. Voices bring me back and through my kitchen door I see cars parked in Maeve's drive. I am tempted to call and ask what has brought them all here. But I am an outsider. I start my coffee and keep an eye out the window.

When I venture into the main room, I see that all three drawings of Franny's Charles have blown off the table and are scattered across the floor. It could have been the night's wind—I had opened my windows some before going to bed. Don't worry, I tell myself.

Still I do worry. I burn my tongue on my coffee, feel an unfamiliar pinch in my lower back, chew on a pencil wishing it were a cigarette from my days of old. If ghosts never leave, then I may be cursed to share this small cottage forever. Worse, if ghosts do not exist, as much of the literature says, if I am thinking my way through this as I mentioned, then I am somehow causing the commotion myself, conjuring my own tribulations, my own weird drama. Losing my mind.

What will happen in winter when I am tucked in tightly with Franny Hale for months on end, continually rearranging her art work like a madwoman, muttering to figments, spinning life stories out of smoke and air as I watch for the lake's ice to crack and melt away? What will I be then, escaped from a reasonable life into this cascade of pink flowers on my wall and the essence of a woman who has taken lead?

There was a time, I might have been seven or eight years old, when I was disciplined to ride my Schwinn Hollywood on just the block where I lived, not to take it any farther, not cross a street or, god save me, ride on the street. And so I went around and around and around, making myself the center of various escapades happening for me in a wooded forest land or in France or some great city like New Orleans, without my ever crossing a street. I invoked tales, made up songs and rhymes and recipes for weird breads with stuff in them like bacon or tomatoes, sometimes even rescuing myself from pretend mayhem and death.

One side of my block faced the elementary school, a three-story brick building with the symmetry that schools had in those days. The top floor was more an attic than part of the school, no classes were held there that I knew and the door to the single stairway accessing that third floor was always closed. On one of my rides past, I noticed a ghost in the center attic window, white and rounded with two gaping black eyes. Like a Halloween costume.

I doubted myself, even then I doubted myself, and so I studied it on many circles of the block before deciding I was right, that the ghost was lonesome and needed discovery. Rules were specific about who could go where in that school and the astute, well-educated women who taught us ensured that these rules were enforced at all times. Nobody wandered about willy-nilly in my elementary school.

I had something of a lisp then, nothing I noticed—nor my mother who thought this diagnosis some sort of bunk. Once a week I climbed the creaking wooden stairs leading to the school attic and met with a speech therapist. There were several small rooms up there where originally the teachers had lived I supposed, all quite bare by the time I was in school, used for music lessons and other one-to-one meetings like mine with the speech therapist. I did not report to a room on the side of the building where my ghost looked out begging to escape, but on my next appointment I found that room. There was the window, large and low in the wall, and in front of the window was a radiator, rounded and white with black gaps between the ironwork looking oddly like eyes.

I don't remember if I had told any friends about the ghost in the attic window and so I can't say if I had to explain my error, endure the common childhood humiliation of being wrong and overly imaginative.

It's not the same as Franny Hale, I tell myself, but my words offer little reassurance.

I find three tiny nails and pound Franny's drawings of Charles into the wood of my mantel, hammering until the nail heads are flush and tight so that no gust of wind will be able to move them. I like how they look. There you go, Franny, I say without saying. Then I gather her other sketches and secure them inside seed catalogs which I stack in one corner of the book shelf alongside the fireplace.

I am taking steps to carry on here in my own way, letting radiators be radiators.

Then I open all windows to let in the morning air.

Then I march up the hill to walk the busy road.

# 19

## Now Where Would I Go?

I see that Maeve has left me messages. The first says hello and little else. In the second call she wonders where I am and repeats that wondering and coughs in a tired way and hangs up forgetting to say goodbye. Then she calls back to tell me she's sorry she forgot to say goodbye and that this morning's nurse is her least favorite. She mutters "oh darn" at something on her end, then asks me to please call and tell her I am fine. There is one more call from her, but no message.

I come up onto Maeve's deck hoping to find her sitting outside on this warm day with the rain-washed sky, but she is not there and the windows have not yet been opened. As soon as I'm at the screen, Eddie howls a greeting from the other side, his black eyes searching mine for some answer to the madness of his life lately. Jimmy hurries to let me in, tells me it's been a hectic day. One of his sisters brought food, the doctor came by for a home visit, the nurses changed shifts midday and he's been in and out with supplies. Now his mother wants him to mow her lawn. As Eddie attaches himself to the side of my leg, I slowly walk toward my friend in the wheelchair.

Maeve's hair is unkempt, a sure sign of trouble in older people I've come to understand, and she has misplaced her glasses, which is the cause of the immediate commotion. She has not had a shower, I think, and nobody thought to put shoes on her feet.

Turning slightly toward me, she raises herself up an inch or two in the chair before saying, "Floria, my dear, you are a sight for sore eyes. Can you believe what's come of me here?" She sounds feisty.

I ask what she'd like me to do and she answers, "Pull this boat straight up onto the shore, that's what." This makes me laugh and then she laughs and Eddie barks, one small gesture triggering the rest. I crank open the two large windows facing the lake and pull over a footstool to sit with her. Jimmy's getting the mower going out there, bucket hat on his head pulled down at an angle.

"He's something, my Jimmy. Oldest children in families seem to take the reins, don't you think? Did you?" I must have tried, I say, working to recall how much sway I might have held over anyone back then. "Well, I'm sure I did too," Maeve says, then nods toward her son. "You know we hadn't planned on him at the time. Not that it was a bad time, but I had other plans I believe. Whatever they were. Eight children and all that time, you get so busy you forget what you set out to do in the first place."

"Raising eight children seems like plenty to do. I cannot imagine."

"Well, it is plenty to do. Of course, I always had help. One housekeeper stayed for so many years she finally got too old for the work. At least that's what I thought. But she never thought she was too old for the work no matter how hard it was for her to take the stairs, up she'd go slow as molasses in January. Mrs. Schreiber. Good German stock she was, refusing to say it was time to call it quits. She'd walk a half a mile to our house six days a week in all weather, there she'd be coming through the door in her green felt hat. Hottest day in July and in would come Mrs. Schreiber, felt hat square in its place, held there with a hat pin maybe four inches long. My goodness, she was something." She gives me a smile. "She'd come to this country as a child and always thought she'd go back to Germany for a visit. But it never happened."

We're quiet together watching Jimmy crisscross her lawn. "I never went to Europe myself," she says suddenly. "Just don't care to fly. If I can't make a trip by car or train, then I don't want to go. And now where would I go? I can barely get to the bathroom. It's something to think about, Floria."

"I think you'll rebound, Maeve. This is just a hurdle."

"That it is."

A minute later she asks me to get the afternoon nurse for help with a shower. "I might at least pretend I'm living a normal life here." I excuse myself from Maeve to find the nurse, who is putting clean sheets on the bed, and I ask that she help my friend take a shower, that I think Maeve's hair needs a comb and that Maeve needs a change of clothing, perhaps a sweater without residue food particles.

The nurse is very young and could use a comb herself. Throughout my suggestions she listens from the other side of the bed. Now she asks, "And who are you?"

"I'm her best friend," I answer, because in this moment I believe that is true, and when the young woman wheels Maeve off to the shower, I decide that as her best friend, I should do something around her house too. With Eddie at my heels, I clear and wash dishes, toss tissues away and give fresh water to the cabbage roses on the piano. I do not, however, close the piano books or cover the keyboard.

Nor do I leave. I choose to stay with Maeve through the remains of this day. I think to tell her about my own trips to Paris, London, Rome, and Stockholm, among other interesting places in Europe, to take her on a few brief expeditions where she does not have to travel by airplane. Or even worry about booking a room.

And just before the sun fades away, so do I, riding a wave of recollections, primeval streets rambled, the ghosts of other days full color in my mind.

# 20

## Here's To You

When I returned from Maeve's on Saturday evening, I found the cottage still and calm as it was when I first moved here. I slept well, remembering no dreams, and woke Sunday to the lake dashing madly against the shore. I mowed, pushing into the wind, until my lawn matched Maeve's. I saw her children and grandchildren come and go, two of them venturing out in the rowboat for much of the afternoon.

Later I sat in one of my porch chairs alternately reading, observing, and napping until the sun dropped across the lake in a magnificent flare. It may seem a small life just now, almost without purpose, certainly without ambition or any of the impatience that ambition brings. But I am surprisingly engaged. The owl that hoots during these daylight hours, various shifts of air currents, clouds that gather and disperse like ethereal neighbors chatting at the corner, the gulls' antics. There are voices bouncing off the water, as I've mentioned before, and laughter. Many afternoons, I catch the smell of smoke from someone's grill or fire pit. Barefoot, I dig my feet into the grass here, wade into the water, pad around on my old wooden floors.

These days I don't find time or the passing of time to be linear or mysterious. A woman with a high ponytail glides by in a canoe around ten on Sunday morning, as she did the day before and probably will again today. It's a circular, momentary existence, something I have not known before.

Once on a visit home, my parents took me to a popular Italian restaurant, standard fare, checkered tablecloths and Chianti bottles. Toward the end of the meal, when my mother had roamed across the room to greet one of her friends, my father said to me—and I no longer remember the exact context—he said life is a flower. That brief, that fleeting. He was not much of a reader and I had never heard him speak a metaphor. He was in his mid-fifties then, had lost both parents and two of his best friends. His children had lives of their own, his hair was thinning, his knees talking back to him now and then, and he was nearing the end of his working years. Life is a flower.

Like Maeve he was seeing a kind of end, a moment when the rose petals would drop from the stem or begin to brown or bow low. And it's something I have held on to all these years, my father's bit of poetry back then. Now here I am living in the end to end, in time on top of time. The rhythm of the lake returning, the cabbage roses planted more than a hundred years ago returning, this old cottage maintaining, Franny Hale still speaking—and my father, too, for that matter. One moment remembering another. How many years from now will Maeve's piano tunes roll through my mind, clear and determined, achingly light despite her hurting hands?

I did not meet up again with Franny Hale all weekend and now it is Monday morning, the last week of June. Waiting for Bo Linney to arrive, I measure the gaping screens on my doors, knowing it is time to fix them before the bugs of July and this is what I am attempting when his van inches down the drive.

"Me again," he says, heading to the lake with his lunch pail and tool bag.

"You ever do small projects, Bo? Mend door screens, that sort of thing?"

"I can do that for you," he says. "Happy to help, just don't tell Harold about it."

"Should I go into town and buy the screening then?"

"Sure, why not?" His focus is on the work he did Friday and I see he barely knows what I'm saying.

And, in fact, his van blocks my drive so I cannot leave for town. I finish my measuring, go inside to do some laundry, sweep the porch, keep busy because Bo is here busy, and when I notice that he's hauled out his dented thermos, I pour myself coffee and go down to the shore to join him.

I ask what he did over the weekend.

He tells me he's working on a play, that there's a community theater in the next town over and they might let him produce his play come winter. "It's a one-act," he says. "Just two main characters, though I might add a chorus to chant, kind of fun, involve more people."

When I ask if he plans to act in his play, he takes a gulp of coffee and nods. "Thought I would actually. Who better, right?" He glances sideways at me. "You want the other lead?"

I laugh, a bit too loud. "I've never been in a play in my life."

"But you can act. I see that. Some people are expressive types, you can just tell."

"How interesting." I don't believe him, but it is an interesting notion. "Who are the two lead characters?"

"One's Macbeth and one's a cleaning lady. But really she's Death."

"You're kidding."

"No, I am not. It's before Macbeth dies and after he's murdered Duncan and Banquo. He's got power in his grip, right? Then he meets up with a castle cleaning lady, minding her own business, but knowing everything that has happened and is about to happen. Like the witches but different." He puts his thermos away and returns to working in his graceful and systematic manner.

We do not talk again today and when he packs up and heads home, I drive to the hardware store for screening. Harold is not working; a skinny kid with several earrings helps me out. I buy a bundle of firewood while I'm at it and a new broom as well.

Now I take the time to cook an entire dinner, set myself up nicely at the table and sit where I can watch the sky transform across the lake. The sketches of Charles seem to follow my every move such that when I finally pick up my glass of wine, I understand I must nod in his direction and include him in my toast. Here's to you, Charles, I say. Whoever you were. He does not converse with me however.

Nor I with him.

# 21

## By The Pricking Of My Thumbs

I dream about Macbeth, but he looks nothing like Bo Linney nor the actor I saw play the role at the Albery Theatre in London years ago. Rather he is a shadow, as illusory as Franny Hale, the unrest obvious, a picking at his airy garments, a dodging of his ghostly head. The dream wrenches me from sleep, filled with suspicion and dread as if I am the one who murdered a kindly king.

It's a clear night, the moon new and high just now. Taking stock, I find nothing amiss on my walls, nothing scattered onto the floor, nothing unearthly here. Out my kitchen window I see lights on at Maeve's, almost every light it seems, and then something moves in the overgrown raspberry bushes between our yards. I swear I'm seeing a bear out there, on its hind legs, but doing what? Eating berries? Are there already berries on my bushes?

I recall that my grandmother's rows of raspberries appeared in June, around this time of the month, and lasted into September, a variety continually producing, at least from my child's perspective. She would walk the rows, a cotton cap covering her head of thinning hair, a coffee can fashioned with a long handle of old rope around her neck, dropping berries into the can, an occasional one popped into her mouth.

I watch the bear now, if it is a bear, nibbling then crouching, then waddling away to where I cannot guess. Woodlands nearby perhaps or berry bushes more ripe and plentiful than my own. When he or she has completely disappeared into the backyard shadows, I escape out the front porch and hurry to Maeve's. Up close I see that an ambulance is parked by the back door and, at this moment when I arrive, Maeve is being carried along, her stretcher eased into the vehicle. I hear the quiet voices of the emergency workers but not what they say. None of her children are present, only a woman I do not recognize—possibly one of her nurses.

Standing on the stairs to her deck and hidden by night, I am in a ridiculous situation, not saying anything because it is not my place, yet unable to move, leave, help. I stay this way as the ambulance slowly departs, its top light circling. In almost the same moment, the attending woman also leaves, locking the door as she goes.

I do not know what any of this means. I'm trying to recall if I saw Maeve move or speak as she was carried to the van, but the night is dark and I was not near enough.

When I was a child, an ambulance came twice for my grandfather who lived next door. His first heart attack occurred without warning. He'd eaten a Dairy Queen cone that day, a Sunday afternoon ritual, and he blamed the cone. The ambulance got him to the hospital in time, but not much could be done in the era before stents, pacemakers, and the like. His doctor told him to drink less wine, which was not good news for an Italian who made his own, and he lived another year, maybe two, before his heart stopped him again, late in the night like this hour now, this place between darkness and dawn, and that second time there were delays, winter weather, a poor phone connection, my grandmother's limited English skills asking for help.

It was my first encounter with loss, though my brother and I were too young to be part of the gatherings and noisy, smoky storytelling. We only knew that our grandfather was no longer living next door. The following summer my parents and grandmother planted his expansive garden at half its former size and that October my father made wine by himself.

This is what I know of ambulances. One saved a life and one did not. But surely Maeve is still alive. Her children aren't here, were not called to the scene, and the woman caring for her left without obvious emotion.

A single lamp remains on by her front screened window and I walk over to stand underneath, look up at the top edges of the piano and her recliner. That's when I hear Eddie alone inside, whimpering long and low because Maeve has gone off without him. I call to him and he stops crying, appears at the screen and, reaching on his hind legs, looks out at me.

"She'll be back, Eddie," I say and scratch at the screen in assurance.

But dogs are not so readily fooled. He barks furiously until it is clear I cannot change his situation, cannot deliver Maeve home where she belongs, then he goes away, leaving me to the wide yard alone, the dread I awoke with now justified, the chant of bad omens loud in the silent night.

# 22

## For Sparrows Fly Unthinking

Nobody brought Maeve home the next day or the next and nobody let me know where she was, what had happened, what I might do or expect. I searched my phone for her daughter's earlier message, but I must have deleted it and so I have no number to call. Tuesday morning, I reappeared at the screen to see Eddie again, but the window had been pulled shut and the house left in stillness.

So something happened. In the early hours, someone came for Eddie and locked down the house, though I should have heard a car in the drive, doors slamming, surely Eddie barking his greeting. But whatever happened, it was without a trace. I cannot say how sad this makes me feel.

Bo Linney continues his work. When the last plank of my dock is set in place, he coaxes me into jumping off the far end to celebrate. He has a towel ready for me—as rough and thin as the ones I use for rags—and a great laugh as well. "Now you can swim with the big fish," he says as he collects his tools.

"I'm just happy to have my own spot to moor," I answer. My new dock is like the cottage's concrete foundation, like my grandmother's sheets, my mother's dishes, my father's voice. Anchors. Rudders. Call it what you will when you feel secured in high winds and rugged circumstances, when you have your place and are sure of it.

After my plunge into the lake, Bo and I sit for a bit, neither of us saying much, just watching the boats and birds. "A heron," he calls, suddenly spotting a great blue lumbering over the water. "Love how they haul those legs around, don't you? Most graceful clunky creatures I know."

I tell him he should live by a lake, that he is meant for this kind of setting.

"Well, we'll see," he answers, like an old man afraid to push his luck too far beyond whatever it is. Then he repeats, "We'll see" to himself and leaps up to move things into his van. "Let's take a look at those screens," he says and spends the rest of the afternoon packing up one project and getting ready to do the next.

Bo is a man who figures things out, his mind as agile as his thin frame. He finds gaps in the porch structure, rot in two of the windows I've already painted. He replaces a rusted drain spout, starts on the screens for both doors. His skills are a marvel really, which I have chosen to observe without much comment other than a small fret over the cost of his time. He shrugs this off. "We'll work it out."

He comes and goes as he is juggling two other projects—a dock repair he deems tedious and a deck on the other side of the lake, a referral from a guy who knows a guy. Not a referral from Harold. "Harold likes my work, but he doesn't particularly like my style," Bo tells me.

"He thinks you're too direct for some of the pampered types around the lake."

"Yeah, direct all right. Harold gives everyone the benefit of the doubt. Loves the whole world. I'm more like that sparrow over there, see him scrapping away and happier for it?" The bird in my drive does not heed the compliment, but continues to peck around for something interesting. "That's okay. I do fine with folks who aren't afraid of a little attitude now and then. Kissing you-know-what has never been my thing."

I think about what Bo calls "attitude." He's never been rude. He just keeps to his own pace and his own mind and if he chooses not to talk much, I have never cared. But he is different from most of the people I've known, who, by and large, hold to social graces. My husband would chat with anyone who engaged him, even at the gas station, even when he wasn't feeling well, even when we were already late for our dinner reservation. He couldn't help himself. And I see that this Bo Linney can't help himself in the opposite direction. I am not like either of them. I extend when I feel a connection. Otherwise I am quiet and people have tended to be fine with that. Possibly I'm not interesting enough for them to bother much about me.

Each time Bo bumps his way up the drive and away, the feelings of my Macbeth dream creep back, this sense of unrest and undoing, that something is not right. Yet through all these days Franny Hale has been absent, long enough for me to think that possibly I made her up in the first place, that some preternatural instinct caused me to see paintings askew when they weren't or imagine her face when it was never there. Lake breezes might be at play here, I begin to believe, or shifts in the ground too subtle for me to observe but real enough to tip things on end.

I do not miss Franny. I miss Maeve though, like I've known the woman all my life and cannot bear being separated from her, and I miss Eddie who is a cheerful dog—coming to me like I've known him all my life too. This week I've also missed Bo whenever he is not here. Last evening, I threw out bread crumbs just to watch the eager sparrows go crazy at my door, fighting over little bits of bread, bold and brave and continually in motion to get what they mean to get.

Now it is Friday, June is ending, and Bo is heading to the North Shore Highlands, the highest falls in the state, he says, with waters that cascade into a gorge in such glory it will refuel his spirit for months to come. Since he moved to the state, he makes this journey every summer over the Fourth of July and this year is no exception. He has his gear packed and a canoe strapped to the roof of his van when he stops by to tell me his plan. His eyes jump around as though he's already searching for the river, almost there though it is hundreds of miles away.

And then he is gone.

I grab a pillow and stretch out on my new dock, stare upward at the fast-moving clouds. A storm is coming. I see it in the sky and I hear it in the wild cries of the birds, their anxious communication to take shelter before the rain.

But I stay until the rumble is loud enough to silence all other lake sounds and I feel the first drops on my skin. Even then, I go only as far as my front porch, where I sit on one of the old chairs, hug my pillow, and wait to see what will come.

# 23

## Storm's Swell

The night is squally now, a summer storm that brings a memory so vague, it is almost in black and white, in sweeps of gray wind and darker gray water. Another inland lake, a screened porch with two daybeds covered in striped cotton blankets, sheets of rain slamming the wooden screen door, more warped than the ones I have here, and someone squealing to go inside, abandon the beds, close the windows.

It wasn't a cabin or hardly a cabin, slumping into the ground, lacking paint, the outhouse some feet from the door and a pump at the sink. I was barely old enough to recall, but we talked about it for years, how we lived weekends at that shack on Dewey Lake just miles from home, a place for the Italian relatives to play bocce, picnic on the grass. A dream of some kind to be Americans on a little lake, one of too many lakes to count that dot the northern landscape.

My father owned it for not even three years. Eventually it became more another lawn to mow and less a prize. The structure unsound, the beach unfit for children, and all of it extra work for my mother who needed to cook ahead of time, pack up the food, haul the linens every weekend. They could not afford a boat or a dock and the fishing from shore turned out to be lacking. Some uncle or cousin spotted a bear on more than one occasion, which terrified my grandmother who had not endured two weeks crossing an unruly ocean only to be eaten by a woodland bear.

Still, she made the drive out every summer Sunday, wearing a dress and brimmed hat and trying to keep herself from telling my grandfather how to drive. I still have a photo of all the family, *la famiglia,* sitting on more of those cotton blankets spread over the grass. My grandfather wears suspenders and looks as happy as I remember seeing him. My mother is the only woman in pants. I am turned away from the camera, in my shorts and halter, sporting the boyish haircut my father gave me one night when my unsuspecting mother was off playing bridge.

I've kept that photo. It tells a whole story. Because my only real memory of Dewey Lake is the storm that blew us off our beds on the porch, that fierce pitch of the wind and rain and how someone shrieked though I cannot say who. For a short while my parents tried to live by a lake, if only on the weekends of summer when they had one small child and cars of close relatives arriving to visit.

This is what I think as I sit in my cottage tonight, listening to the storm swell around me, hearing no clear voices from another realm—only the rhythmic banging of a warped screen door decades ago on Dewey Lake.

# 24

## Who Loves The Rain

In the morning, it is Maeve on the phone.

"I've been away you know," she begins, her tone steady. "Another something or other and off they shipped me to the hospital."

I tell her I know, I was on her steps watching. "You gave me a scare," I say.

"They tell me I'm going home in an hour, which I would like to believe. Is it raining, Floria?"

"Raining?"

"There's a curtain around me here. But I heard rain last night, I'm certain I did."

"We had quite a storm, Maeve, but it's done now. The sun is breaking and there's that shimmer off the lake we get in the mornings."

"I knew it had rained. How I hate to miss a thunderstorm on that lake. Not that Eddie loves a storm. But he has his hiding places, Eddie does."

I ask where he is because I know he's not at her house right now.

"Oh. He's with one of the children, I suspect. But nobody said anything to me. It's no wonder I am not getting any better with all this moving from one place to another, Floria. I did not have a stroke, you know. I did not have a heart attack. I did not break any bones and I can see as well and far as ever. So what is the matter here?"

It is not a rhetorical question. She really wants my answer, and so I do my best. "It may be a combination of factors," I say.

"This is not going to be good, Floria."

I say, "No, wait. It might be." I tell her the fall obviously disturbed some inner workings, whatever they are, that I have fallen hard a few times and it seems afterward everything reverberates. "A fall knocks you off-kilter," I add. "Then you add being older, general wear and tear and—" She wants to argue. "No, Maeve, let me finish. They kept you so sedentary. In a wheelchair. How does your blood get going in a wheelchair?"

She's silent.

"Maeve?"

"I'm thinking what to do about this."

"Your nursing people seem afraid to have you move in case you fall again."

"Well, of course. I'm at everyone's mercy now it seems. Children, nurses, doctors, ambulance drivers." She pauses. "I don't suppose you can spring me, can you?"

"Spring you?"

"Invite me to dinner. Just me and Eddie, no helpers, no offspring. Just us, that's it. And I'll insist. I'll say I want to sit at your big table there and ponder the roses on your walls."

"Of course, you are invited, Maeve."

"And I will make it happen. The next time it rains on our lake, I will be front and center to witness it." I respond that this is splendid and begin to say more when she hangs up. Which tells me she's working on her plan already, gearing up to arrange things.

It is the first day of July, both lake and sky pearly. I take Maeve's red boat and row to the mouth of the bay. It's so early that most of the Saturday crowd has not yet appeared with their heavy-duty motors and skiers and tubes and coolers of beer. I won't say it's quiet, but it is almost quiet and I consider Maeve's situation. Being older, beginning to be dependent after a lifetime of not just autonomy but running the whole show, being the mother of eight children, teaching them all, keeping them in line, offering praise and boundaries, being the one to say yes and the one to say no, the one to say this will not do at all. Now at their mercy, as she says. Barely able to make it out of bed on her own. The dismaying shock of finding herself in such a position.

My parents and grandparents did not face that. All, to a person, died while still able to walk, think more or less clearly, and divine their own destinies, even if their joints ached or they forgot birthdays or moved more slowly through their days. They still moved and their days were still their own until the very end. This is the first time I have seen aging as a dreadful loss of independence. It was only three weeks ago that Maeve and Eddie first appeared at my door. She walked over with banana bread she had made and stood with relative ease commenting on my sweet cottage as I renamed myself Floria.

When I turn the boat toward home again, there is Maeve's gray house on the shore next to my small white one, which from this point on the lake, seems to be settling deeper into my bit of land, its screened porch peering out from a cozy depth of the landscape. Distance aids perspective. I see my place how others see it, leaning and low and looking like it is from another century, which is true, and from another form of lake-living, such as my parents' experiment on Dewey Lake, my cottage possibly home to an aging hermit, a scrapping poet, or, as it seems, the ghost of a woman who sketched fruits and flowers.

I tie Maeve's red rowboat to her dock and return home.

Though nothing here has changed in my absence, I feel it has.

I've seen my small home's truth, I fear.

It's weary soul perhaps.

# 25

## A Thousand Watts

Things come together on the Fourth of July. Maeve's children and grandchildren are not invited to picnic on her lawn and race merrily about because she is dining with me, and if it is a production to get her here, it is what everyone wants. A normal social event. A late afternoon chat over summer soup and salad. Her eldest son, Jimmy, wheels Maeve across the bumpy terrain of our yards, up the two steps to my porch and into the cottage. Eddie follows them and finds a spot near the door that affords him a lake breeze.

All windows are open, the air humid and moving through, not unbearable. I have draped the table in a heavy linen sheet bought when I was wandering Paris years ago, and, though the cabbage roses are spent for the season, I've hunted the back hill for bunches of oxeye daisies and some colorful weeds with bits of blossom, even stray twigs fallen from the trees. It's a grand assortment and Maeve notices immediately. As I knew she would.

"Oh, this is lovely, Floria."

We are both delighted, this is true. I have taken out my mother's dishes which Maeve recognizes as something in her past, a neighbor who collected this very pattern, so popular in the day, she tells me. "But when Jim and I were first married I bought my dishes using coupons at the grocery store, a dinner plate if I spent five dollars, something like that. One by one I got a set for twelve along with the cream and sugar containers. We always had those, you know. And serving bowls, even a teapot I believe. All with tiny flowers in the center and edged in a little fake gold."

She has none of them left. "Eight children," she says. "Whatever happened to those kinds of coupons, I wonder. Green Stamps and the like? I miss so many simple things."

The light turns as we are eating until the glow steadies on the sketches of Charles along the mantel. "Now who would that be?" Maeve asks. I explain how I found the drawings in my shed and believe them to be the work of the previous owner who also did the paintings along the wall near the front door.

"Do you like looking at them, Floria?"

"I think she was a good artist," I say, but I understand this isn't quite what she's asking. I do not want to explain that hanging the sketches of Charles across my mantel is a form of appeasement in my mind. That ever since I pounded them there I have not heard from nor seen Franny Hale.

That is about to change.

Not at the moment of Maeve's question, but now, as the sun slides farther toward the lake and the corners of the room fall to shadow. Outside, the first fireworks of the night explode, and I take a last bite of the bread I put out to accompany our meal. Maeve is still studying the sketches of Charles, Eddie sleeps deeply on the rug, and Franny appears. Suddenly, soundlessly, weird and unsettling as ever.

Maeve says, "Oh," and looks over to me to affirm that something is truly before us.

"It's Franny Hale," I say in a hush. Eddie stays still, not seeming to sense the presence of a ghost in the room as Franny Hale floats near her sketches. Maeve stares straight at her and I hold my breath. I'm waiting for Franny to dissipate as she always does.

Except this time, she does not, at least not for a longer while. We remain a tableau. Nothing moves except the loose ends of the Charles sketches, which respond to Franny as if to a light draft of air lifting the edges of the paper. I see that the delicate stems of wild flowers are doing the same, swaying just barely, and a wisp of Maeve's hair as well, loose and lifting.

Then there is no more image, no more bit of breeze. Eddie

raises his head as if from a dream before tucking himself together more tightly. "Goodness, Floria, what just happened?"

"I thought she'd finally left for good."

Maeve takes in the entirety of my rooms, turning not only her head but her wheelchair too. "I don't see why she would," she says.

Before I say anything more, I light the candles on top of the mantel and two smaller ones on the table near us. Then I venture to explain. How Franny has been visiting me since my second week here, how she has blown things to the floor, tipped her own paintings, swayed before me at this very time of evening when the last of the sun is fading. But never a sound and never a clear signal as to what she wants. "Sometimes afterward, Maeve, I am left with such a sense of longing, something I cannot explain. She had a good life," I say. "I'm told she died easily, in her garden, putting it to rest for the winter. The man who owns the hardware store in town told me this. So it's hard to understand, you know, why she stays or has returned. Why is she here?"

Outside, fireworks are popping one after another and Eddie whines, scoots under the table to sit at Maeve's feet. "I can't believe what I just saw," she says. "I simply would not have believed."

"I haven't seen her in days and was beginning to think she was a figment, that I made her up somehow."

"Obviously, that is not so," Maeve says.

"Maybe I've left the place too much the way she knew it. When I moved in, the three paintings were hanging right where they are and, of course, this wallpaper has been here since god knows when. I just plopped down a few pieces of furniture and began to carry on. The cabbage roses bloomed. Now the raspberries are starting. Other than a few repairs and some painting, I think this house is the same as it was when she died thirty-some years ago."

"That long?" Maeve is calculating the heft of the years. At the time when Franny Hale died, Maeve was running a full household, volunteering for community activities, driving here and there in some big, safe, kid-friendly car. "Goodness, she's determined."

I shrug. "She could be some ancient spirit of the land. I've researched this phenomenon. Even if the place burned to the ground, she'd stay. Some drunk teenager roaring by in a motorboat would ask his buddies what the hell is that light floating along the shore?"

There's an explosion of fireworks suddenly and Eddie barks in fright. I pick him up, place him on Maeve's lap, and roll them out to my porch where we stay watching sprays and sparkles bursting and falling away into the water. Then, like Franny Hale, all is gone, the show is done and we hear only faint laughter from the other side of the bay.

"It's been such a night, Floria," Maeve says as I pull her wheelchair up the stairs to her deck. A caretaker is there to meet me, and Eddie hustles inside to find his favorite pillow. I hold Maeve's hand for a moment, or she holds mine, and I say, "Indeed, it has been such a night."

# 26

## O Lonely Tree

My Italian grandmother came to this country in her late teens, at what exact age I do not know. After spending two weeks on a ship and another week on a train to the Midwest, she chose never to return. Even when my grandfather traveled there to find out how his relatives were spending the money he had been sending them. Even when her niece invited her to fly on an airplane to visit their village. She did not express any need or interest, not ever, my mother told me, until my grandmother had her first stroke. This caused some confusion, limited her activities, and clearly signaled a denouement.

At a Sunday gathering in her kitchen, my father got my grandmother telling tales of old. About the sheep on the hillside. Her father's home with its tiled floors and wrought-iron gate. About leaving school though she was more quick than any of her brothers. As she talked, her face grew flush, almost fevered, to remember everything she remembered. "I think," she said to my mother, "I think I lika go back."

I had gone home to see my grandmother that weekend and so was there to hear her make that declaration and to watch my mother, beleaguered by my grandmother's stroke and its consequences, as she turned from the sink where she stood scraping dishes. "Ma," she said without patience, "now's a fine time to think of that."

And so my grandmother in her nineties did not return to Italy to see the rolling mountains where she had tended sheep. She died a month later. It is for me to consider now if her persistent energy, the same that kept her going in a foreign country where only relatives from her exact village understood her dialect, the same that held her to high standards, tidy dress, intricate lace, and pasta just as elegant, if this same resolution took her back despite my mother's dismissal and the cold fact of death. What if, like Franny, my grandmother made her return? What if her after-journey brought her to the tiny place of her childhood where the scent of mountain air is more than memory?

It is late. July Fourth has become July fifth and here I am wondering about things unknown, what longing draws anyone to another place, another dimension, how willful, beset or charmed must one be to have this other journey, to tip paintings on end and waft through at evening? Why has my husband never come by? Not even when I wear his old woolen shirt?

Since Maeve left, I have kept a lamp on by my chair and soon that bit of glow will be overcome by daylight. If I sleep now, it's without realization. If Franny reappears, it's nothing I see or sense. I hear my father telling me, as he always tells me, that I think too much. It's not worth the trouble.

# 27

## By Any Other Name

Maeve calls first thing and here I am, still in my chair. She wants to report how well she slept, the satisfaction of having an evening with me. "Today I'm going to park my wheels by the lake and watch the world go by," she says with enthusiasm. "Join me if you like." Then I hear another voice talking and our call quickly ends.

It is not natural to spend all night in a chair, even a squashy one like mine. When I stand up, I am so stiff I get a momentary sense of what Maeve means when she talks about her arthritis. "This is not an illness, Floria. It is a situation." Now something like that gives me trouble until I walk it off, from the back door to the front and down to my dock. As I stretch, perched like a lonely gull at the edge of the dock, I hear "Hi ho," coming from my driveway.

Bo is back from his reset, has been driving since just past midnight to make it here in time, he says.

"In time for what?" I ask.

"July fifth," he answers. "Reporting for duty."

The windshield of his van is splattered with bugs, he's shaggier looking than usual and reeks to high heaven. "I don't mind if you go home first," I say, but he'll have none of it.

"Breaks the spell," he tells me and gets back to repairing my screens. He sings under his breath like a man in love, like a man experiencing the deluded euphoria of love. "Maybe next year you can drive up with me," he calls out from the back step. "Separate tents, of course," he adds and grins. "It's not just what you see there, it's the feel of the spray, the sense of height, those rocks hot under your feet." After this lyrical assessment, he goes back to his songs, whatever they are.

Standing on the other side of the screen, I say, "You have a nice voice."

"Maybe I should turn my one act into a musical."

I say he can count me out then. I can't even do a simple scale.

"Nobody wants to listen to a simple scale anyway, Floria Whoever You Are." He grins again, full of good humor this day after his epiphany at the northern edge of the country. I make us an early lunch with leftovers and watch as he eats what I put out—every slice, berry, and crumb. We sit on the steps looking toward my back hill with its midsummer flowers and rampant undergrowth, and I notice the largeness of Bo's gestures. His hands are bony and long and move dramatically to finish the last crust of his sandwich.

"You're an artist," I say.

"That's true. I am an artist in search of an art. You?"

"Not so much," I answer. "But just living can be a kind of art, attending to the quality of things, goodly details like the lace on my grandmother's sheets."

He chews and stares at me like a contemplative cow. "What's your name really?"

This is where the conversation ends. I brush the bits of bread from my lap and tell him that some things are better left unsaid.

"Why?"

"Pull the loose thread and you might unravel the whole cloth."

"A rose by any other name," he counters.

I raise my eyebrows and go inside. Whatever I am doing here, with my history, my stories collected along the way, and habits and notions, there is no putting it all together. No piece over here fitting into the piece over there. At this time in my life I am more a jumble sale, a merry old mishmash of people, places, and loves, and I am unwilling to relinquish the scramble. I need, as it were, the mystery.

I hear the doors of Bo's van opening and slamming closed,

hear his boots on the gravel drive. "I'm heading out," he hollers through the screen. "See you after noon tomorrow." He's singing again as he gets into his van, so not knowing my name has apparently had little effect on his mood. The powerful waterfalls are still filling him full.

Then the air changes, as it does each time Bo departs. Not because he's loud. He rarely speaks and then only in single sentences or fragments of sentences. But his presence fills considerable space. Maybe it's the noisy tools, maybe the lifting and shifting and movement, but probably more his character which is whole and hardy. Now things settle again, even the dust on the drive. The sky this moment is without clouds, the raspberry bushes heavy, the breeze barely noticeable.

Even quiet places are not quiet. A board creaks or cracks, power comes on, shuts off, a tree branch scratches against a window somewhere close. If none of these, then at least the heart pulses, faint perhaps. But persistent.

705-059-395-324- 2

# 28

## Every Gust & Drop

I catch Maeve's laugh before I see her sitting at the shoreline. Two of her daughters are on the grass beside her and Eddie, of course, but I hesitate to join them. They are family and I am not. I see the two sisters with shoulders touching—their heads cocked at the same angle, hair color nearly indistinguishable. I come from a line of only-girl children. My Italian grandmother had brothers, my mother the same, and I, too, have a brother and no sisters.

I cannot say now if my grandmother or mother missed the presence of sisters. I think I have not. But there are times, like today, when I watch the chumminess of Maeve's daughters and feel uncomfortably separate. As close as friends may get, they are not the ones who shared a bedroom and hand-me-downs and laughed hysterically with you in the back seat of the family car for no reason whatsoever. Friends did not have the same Aunt Marguerite, Jean, or Evelyn who smoked and drank cocktails, nor did they grow up eating the same dread zucchini pancakes midsummer. I often noticed how friends' older sisters knew things that parents seemed not to know and were ever eager to enlighten their younger sisters. Dirty words and French kissing come to mind, and how to wear socks in line with the trend, and when to choose pink lipstick and when to choose red.

So I stay on my porch until Maeve and Eddie are alone before I stroll over. The air has changed since morning, the almost nonexistent breeze now billowing and becoming energetic.

"I'm going to get my rain," Maeve announces. "I'll watch it come and I'll stay at my window through every gust and drop."

I remark that it's only wind, to not get her hopes up.

"But I feel it," she says with a dreamy gaze outward. "Eddie does, too, don't you, sweet dog? See how his tail twitches? That's rain on the way."

I sit on the grass next to her wheelchair as the wind brings the clouds in overhead, high and traveling quickly.

"Did your ghost return last night?" she asks.

"I don't think so, but I slept in the chair by the mantel just in case."

"Just in case? My goodness, you are not in charge, Floria, you know. This face in the room will come and go as she pleases. I must say, I would not have believed it if I hadn't seen her myself."

I ask if she thinks I should be frightened, should hire some sort of fumigator. Or exorcist. This comes out sounding so ridiculous we both laugh.

"In my life," Maeve says, "I've never had much time for speculative folderol. Always too busy. Even these last years, I'm busy. Then you're near the end and who wants to waste precious time wondering this or that, life after death, the soul's journey, Jesus at the gate?" She shrugs. "Who's to know. I'm a believer, but even believers don't believe everything. Yet there it is, you have a ghost and I saw her myself."

I ask what she thinks that proves.

"Something," she answers. "It must prove something. I'd like to ask her a few questions. Find out what's what."

Just then the wind blows Maeve's tissue off her lap and sends it tumbling across the lawn. She lifts her arms into the gusty air and calls out, "This is just where I want to be. Bring it on, right, Eddie?"

The dog is not so sure and growls under his breath, ears hanging low. I point out the features of my new dock to Maeve, its wood not yet weathered, and tell her about what's blooming around my yard. I say I'll bring some raspberries over to her soon.

"You're a good neighbor," she tells me. I say likewise, and

we feel the first of the rain she is waiting for, faint drops at first and then more.

"I think I need to get you inside," I yell, but she says not yet, not yet until we are both wet and Eddie is tugging at his leash. When the day's caretaker comes across the lawn for her, Maeve loses the moment. I hurry along next to them chattering something about looking out at the rain from inside her house and Maeve keeps her face open to the pelting until she is through the door and the door is closed behind her.

I am soaked. No part of me is dry and the sky has quickly darkened to twilight. I make my way back across the lawn, then turn to see Maeve at her front screen, arms again wide to the weather.

Being alive is this. The exhilaration of a sudden storm and the water turning gray and wild. The waves crash toward me leaving foam on the shore. Boats are gone, the lake left to its essence, one with the rain and the wind, dark as the sky. I do not want to leave it any more than Maeve did. I am wet anyway and so I stay. I stretch out on my dock and take what comes. It is at least a half hour before I pull myself up and go inside.

I peel my clothes off on the porch and drape them over the old wooden chairs, drip my way to the bathroom and wrap my robe around me, then a blanket on top of the robe. The cottage was warm the past few days, but this wind is blowing such that I need to shut a few windows. I reheat what's left of the morning coffee and snack on a cracker.

Why do I forget to look for Franny?

She's been here. In my absence, she has come to tip her paintings again, an old trick revisited. Seeing this jolts me from my reverie of weather and time, living and dying. Franny is none of that to me. She is not a symbol of the everlasting as Maeve thinks. She makes herself so present, so active and part of my routine that I struggle to remember Franny is a ghost.

I straighten the pictures, dust the tops with my thumb. No matter how much Franny upsets or annoys me, I never stop loving her paintings. Each of them draws me in as though I am the one in the sailboat, the woman walking the beach, as though I might live high on an ocean-side cliff in a house with a roof that is red. I step back to get the best angle and then it occurs to me that maybe this moving of the pictures is something of a discourse. Hello and hello. My move, your move. An ongoing game of sorts.

It's such a thought.

Like Bo this morning, I begin to sing and the songs that come to me are ones I learned a long time ago, songs I heard on my father's radio and never seem to forget.

# 29

## Were They Normal?

The rain lasted all night and now continues against my roof and west windows. I stay under my grandmother's lovely bedding, doubting Bo will show up to work in this weather. But we've never exchanged telephone numbers, so I do not know. I like it when he comes by, look forward to the groan of his van and the bit of commotion he brings. And what if I do become the character Death in his play, dressed as a cleaning lady, my hair pulled up under a scarf, mop in hand, and the wisdom of the ages in my eyes? I'm thinking this through.

He's writing the lines, of course, but eventually, Macbeth will collapse in my arms. Nobody is able to save him. Nobody is able to pull evil out of itself, polish it up, allow it to shine again. Not even an ardent cleaning lady.

But I wonder if doing this play will move me in a direction I don't seek. More people to know, more expectations. Perhaps the theater will want me to take on another project, play the Madwoman of Chaillot or Nora in *A Doll's House*. Wonderful, juicy parts that real actresses play in cities where theater reigns. And then what would I do? And what would I call myself? And where would it end?

Maeve's call startles me out of these wanderings. "Floria," she about shouts into the phone, "isn't this a marvelous rain? I am so pleased to witness this rain, all night and now into the morning. Look outside. There's nobody on the lake. Maybe a loon out there, could it be? Well, I just called to say aren't we so lucky."

I agree with everything she says, even slide out of bed and walk onto my porch so that I see what she sees, the gray lake reflected by the gray sky, no people, and the one lone bird or duck across the bay. "Yes, we are so lucky, Maeve. Would you like me to bring raspberries later? If the rain stops so I can pick them, I'll bring a bowl over for you."

"Well you know I'll be here. Me and my entourage." She laughs, too delighted with the rain to be derisive about her caretakers today. And then the call is over.

It's the first all-day rain since I moved here and the constant rhythm on the roof is raucous in this small space, so noisy I do not hear Bo's van until his brakes squeal to a stop in the drive. He jumps out and waves at me from under a hooded poncho. When I let him in, he stands dripping and says he was driving this way and has come to say hello. I take his poncho and drape it over the washing machine that sits near the back door, then offer to make him coffee.

"Of course," he says, unties his wet boots and shuffles across the floor in speckled workman's socks, the kind my father used to wear and my grandfather as well. He sits at my old table and, without moving anything other than his eyes, he surveys the inside of my cottage, the furniture and book shelves, Franny's paintings and drawings, the fireplace, then over to my tiny corner kitchen where I stand measuring coffee. "Looks like you've lived here forever."

"I did kind of settle in."

"You like to read."

I tell him that I have never stopped reading since the day I found my first five words on the page. I say the books I have here are mostly ones I've already read and cannot part with, only a small few are those I have not yet read. I have collections of mysteries, I say, bought from various mail-in book clubs years ago and also a considerable stack of bird books. I have general reference books that I think essential to any researcher regardless of the internet. I have cookbooks with all my notations and drips of oil or melted chocolate decorating the recipes. Art books, a few anyway.

"What are you reading now?" he asks me.

"I'm reading *Howards End* for the third time. There's a cottage," I tell him. "It's primary to the story," I say, and he nods. But I'm not sure if that means he's read *Howards End.*

"You see the movie?" he asks.

"I saw it more than once and loved it. But the book is something else."

"I brought my script," he says, goes back to his poncho, and takes out a roll of papers. "Want to look at it?" He smooths the pages out on the table and hands them to me. We drink our strong coffee—I forget to ask if he wants milk or sugar—and I read the peculiar conversation he's written between the startled, half-crazed Macbeth and the castle cleaning lady who knows what he has done. She doesn't have many lines, so it won't be challenging to memorize her part. "The play's more physical than verbal," Bo says and stands, unfolding himself into Macbeth. He towers, arms spread and flailing out of control, then contracts inward like he is paranoid, his gaze here and there into the corners where there is nothing to see, behind him, and underneath the table. He's riveting.

"Can't help myself," Bo remarks as he returns to himself, sits at the table, and takes a drink of coffee as if nothing had just happened.

"You really looked crazed, Bo."

"That's the idea. I've been working on it. In the dark hours, of course. Who wants a madman out repairing their dock? Good coffee."

"I think I'm going to do your play."

He nods. "I figured you would."

The rain stops, quite suddenly, and everything falls quiet. Water drips off the roof on all sides of the cottage, almost musical. "I have a ghost," I say.

"Here?"

I summarize my situation in a few sentences and watch his face to see where it goes. "All this artwork is hers," I add.

Like I've said before, Bo Linney is a person who considers things, examines things. If I have a bit of the actress in me, as he says, then I'll venture that he has a bit of the researcher in him. This new information does not change his posture any and he remains relaxed, keeps sipping his coffee. “Pretty strange,” he says at last.

And that it is.

# 30

## Dream Of My First Life

It is not until today, Friday, the air humid and heavy, that Bo declares he'd like to meet Franny Hale. He has finished repairing screens and is laboring over the two window sills when he pauses, comes to the back door, and makes this announcement. I am in the middle of folding my laundry, my mind somewhere else, and his words confuse me for a moment.

"Meet her?"

Bo nods.

I start to laugh. Even to my own ears, there is some hysteria in the laugh, a slightly unhinged aspect to it. "You don't understand," I say. "There's no plan. It's not regular or anticipated, Bo. Things just happen."

"You don't think she'd want to meet me? I mean, if you let her know?"

"And how am I to do that, let her know?"

He's impassive. "I think you could just ask." And without warning, he hollers, "Hello, Franny Hale. How are you?" His voice is so loud, much much too loud, and in immediate response, I slam the inside door shut, leaving Bo on the other side of the screen as startled by my behavior as I am by his. Then I sit at the table to collect myself.

I need to say here that I have spent a lifetime avoiding scenes of any kind. I was raised that way. At this very moment, I see my mother's mouth downturned in disapproval, my father shaking his head, my grandmother's eyes wide in shock. Who yells out like Bo just did, blasting through the sound barrier for the whole neighborhood to hear—or even just my neighbors on the other side of the thicket? No one in my world.

The people of my childhood were mostly not refined. Nor

particularly well-educated, nor saddled by excessive restraint. Mr. Hocking, three houses down, drank during the days when he did not work, which tended to be many days, and often his two kids, nine cats, and chain-smoking wife would push him to the brink. I once saw the man storm out of the house and throw their vacuum cleaner halfway across the lawn, swearing a blue streak. Our next-door neighbor had similar though less frequent rages, which I witnessed and have never forgotten. Even the little wiry grandmother at the far end of our block occasionally chased children with her broom, screaming their real or imagined offenses all the while.

But in my family, none of this was acceptable. Yelling across houses and backyards was not acceptable. Interrupting adults when they spoke or bragging about accomplishments or any obvious demonstrations of large feelings was just not acceptable. Surely hollering hello to a ghost falls into that category.

Bo Linney and I keep to ourselves throughout this day. He works diligently outside and I slip away, walk for miles enduring dust and traffic and return to find him gone. Fine, I tell myself. But it is not how I feel at the sight of my drive, empty except for my own car stowed under the birches.

He's done good work again, one rotted window sill repaired and repainted and the other in process. Surveying this north side of my cottage, I see the berry bushes laden and remember I told Maeve I would bring some over to her, so I head inside for a bowl. It's late afternoon and the westerly light floods my cottage. At a glance, I see that all the paintings are level, my stack of folded clothes ordered nicely atop the washing machine, the bed made to perfection as I am wont to do. Bo's call to Franny Hale failed, I think. Shouting for ghosts to appear does not work.

But, as I turn into the shadows of my tiny kitchen, Franny Hale is there to prove me wrong again. I see her in full this time, shoes even, more like boots, the sort my grandfather and his cronies wore every day. She hovers near my stove, near what was most likely her stove, and she stays and stares, as do I.

I am waiting for the air to clear, for reality to return, Franny to dissipate.

"What?" I say at last. "What is it, Franny?"

She seems to nod or I am imagining that she does, not knowing what it would mean if that were true. "I love it here," I say, as the familiar weightiness takes hold, the restless longing she has led me to before and leads me to now. It is such a beautiful afternoon and the lakeside light so soft. The pink walls glow, they do, and if I had Franny's talent, I would paint this room at this angle and time of evening.

I step back from the kitchen entry and when I do, she dematerializes. Evaporates.

"Bo would like to meet you," I mutter, such a silly thing to say.

She already knows that.

It seems she has answered in kind.

# 31

## Swimming At Night

I try to put it aside. Bring raspberries to Maeve. Drive into town for take-away food, which I eat on the dock. I stay to watch the sun set and the boats putter toward wherever they call home. Voices echo. Laughter, of course. One woman toots into the darkness like a strange bird out there on the water and I am tempted to toot right back at her.

Instead I gather my trash and go inside. I did not leave a lamp on earlier so the only light is what comes from the moon, a narrow shaft that streaks from the screened porch into the main room, the kind of light I might consider romantic under different circumstances. I whisper Franny's name, do not ask me why. Then I turn on the lamp by my chair, sit, and slowly survey my space.

Everything is still.

Everything looks right.

This is a time of day I have always favored. As a teenager, I waited for this hour when all in the house were asleep except for me and the cat. Like now, I'd settle in, contemplate and tell myself whatever I wanted to hear. It was when I came to terms with myself, sorted the impossibilities, wove my wonder so to speak. I went places in the late hours. Alone in my mother's Early American chair purchased with Gold Bond Stamps, I went places. The cat would slam her head into my leg the way cats do when they are claiming a person as their own, rubbing their scent onto you. That was my time.

Tomorrow is Saturday. One month since I moved in. I've driven my car fewer than twenty miles since I parked at the bottom of the hill that day, have had no contact with the life

I lived, have not even heard from my brother who tends to be busy in this season. When I left, I did not consider the people who might await me here, only this bit of property on the lake.

For weeks before I moved, I daydreamed endlessly about the flowered wallpaper and screened porch. I closed my eyes in that city flat and heard the waves, these waves, lapping and slapping to shore. I drew diagrams. Where to put the chairs, the bed, whether or not to take a rug with me or the daybed, my one expensive art print, and if so, where these would go. I transitioned weeks before I landed to unpack my things.

This day comes and passes like the slight clouds overhead, moving yet barely moving. Saturday night is its own wild time on the lake, as it always seems to be, and I swim off my dock, paddle around pretending to be part of things. It crosses my mind to be bold and make my way to Maeve's dock and back. But I do not do this. It's enough to float here near my own shoreline, close to my cottage, my stuff, the gathered stores of my life so far.

Adding it up, I must say I am quite satisfied. I lack *want* just now, a Buddhist sort of notion I've been told, not to want. To float and observe, to work without aspiration. Which may be another reason Franny Hale troubles me. Franny Hale brings with her the energy of want. Of loss and longing. And when I see her, I feel the weightiness of that longing too.

The lake's temperature has risen these past two weeks, as Maeve predicted. I pull myself out only after every boat is gone and I hear the first call of an owl. I won't say that all is quiet, but the weekend noises have dulled to a murmur and an occasional firecracker left over from the holiday. The cottage is warm from the day, and smells, as it does, of wood and smoke and the white pines that surround it. Everything is as I left it.

I find myself drawn into the sketches of the young man named Charles who looks across the room at me with humor and affection.

Come Sunday morning, he is the same.

Come Sunday morning, all is the same, and cars begin arriving at Maeve's. She phones to invite me over for their renewed Sunday picnic in the yard, and I say yes. Her voice is old Maeve, sure and a bit bossy, though when I see her, she does not look any better physically. Her coloring is off in some way and she seems smaller in her wheelchair. But that could be my own faulty perception. I decide to put it to that. I hug her and squat low to chat.

"You were out swimming in the dark last night."

"If you can call it swimming," I say.

"Mother loved swimming at night," one of the daughters shouts out and another starts in about how much they all loved swimming after dark back in the day, which opens a noisy dialogue about their childhood summers at the cabin and the time the youngest almost drowned and great laughs about the canoe kit their father failed to conquer and their water wars with kids from neighboring cabins. They talk over and around one another, something that did not happen in my small and more reticent family. I see my grandmother trying to follow the thread of their talk, this barrage of English words she would not have understood.

And then there is the tale of Maeve sending her youngest daughter up to a stranger's door to ask for gasoline when the car ran out on a drive to their cabin. "You think this kindly woman with her gentlemanly dog was always this way?" They laugh. "She said it would be fine. The lawn was trimmed and the house orderly. Those are the kind of people who give gas to strangers."

"Lesson learned," Jimmy says. "Mother is always right."

They are more involved with her at this party than they were a few weeks back, before she fell and struggled and landed in the hospital two times. She is no longer a given. At any time, she could depart the scene and not return. I see they know this now.

And their stories please her. She looks my way, shaking her head in the familiar delight of her children and their antics. Eddie sits at her side. The clouds are low, the air humid, the lake gentle.

I stay for hours with the Murphy clan, give myself over to their hilarity and geniality. Mostly I sit on the grass by Maeve; we eat together, watch the others and the lake society beyond us, neither saying much. But then, when no one is too close, she asks what is happening with Franny Hale. "I haven't forgotten her," she says. "I still have questions for her, you know."

She looks beyond me.

"It's the direction things are heading, Floria."

# 32

## Commentary Of Crows

Bo does not show early Monday. His other projects, I tell myself. Or the weather possibly, the overcast sky heavy and white everywhere, crows screeching in disapproval. I notice they tend to come forward on days when there is no sun, hollering from tree to tree. Other birds do not speak. I hear none of the soft voices I normally hear—mating and parenting and commenting on the lightness of air. Only crows.

I think they understand inherently, instinctively how they hold the power of myth. How they have been keepers of secrets, creatures of divine light. A crow represented Apollo, after all, who changed its feathers from white to black. So, of course, they have a voice, are not to be sidelined or dismissed.

The thick cloud cover, the crows, the spirit of Franny Hale converge with my own unease as though some forfeiture is pending. Even on a summer day with the grass so green.

No one in my immediate family died in this season. They all exited in bleak months—the end of November, the end of December, the harsh centers of February and March. My mother died as April trailed off and we buried her on May Day. But it was in a northern place where, though the sun shone, the air felt crisp. I wore black wool. But perhaps an aunt died in July. Perhaps an older cousin. Italian relatives, I think, may have chosen to leave only when the tomatoes had begun to ripen and their flowers were at full flush. Like Franny collapsing just as her garden came to its seasonal rest, on a bright day, I'm picturing, with the birch trees here golden and the crows silent.

Thinking this, I walk behind the house, wondering where her garden might have been. Not on the north side with the berries. It's too narrow and there is not enough sun. And not on the south side beneath all the trees. The storage shed is surrounded by grass and weeds which I cut down every week with the old mower, but it seems this must have been her spot, a patch that caught the morning light full-on and the midday sun through early afternoon. It's on a bit of slope, though that might not matter to growing plants. Vineyards are often on hills, the plants tough and intertwined, tidy in rows but not necessarily on level ground.

This is what I'm considering when Bo turns down the driveway, comes over in that lanky way of his and says he just has one small thing to finish up today and he'll be back tomorrow to do the rest. He says nothing of his outburst last week.

"I want to put a garden over there," I say, also choosing to say nothing of his outburst last week. I point to a patch of lawn, draw a large square in the humid air. "I think that's where the original owner had it."

"The ghost?"

"When she was alive. Harold told me she died in the garden. Now there's no garden but I'm pretty sure that's where it was." He asks if I think a garden will make her happy, and I say no, that I think a garden will make me happy.

"Pretty late in the season to get it going," he offers. "But, I don't know. I suppose you could buy some plants already started, turn things over and mulch, see what takes." He's not looking at me. He's staring at the grass where a garden may emerge.

"You have a garden?" I ask.

"No," he says. "No time. But I'd help you. Want me to dig up the grass for you?"

I like this idea. He says he'll take payment in produce and we talk about what I should grow, what would be reasonable to try. We throw out our favorites, carrots and zucchini for him, tomatoes and basil for me. The sky is still low, the crows still loud, but the day takes an upbeat turn, like landing in a new city, getting ready to hit the pavement and see what's what. Bo finds the rusted shovel in the shed and I drive into town for black dirt, compost, and a few plants to start.

Bo does not finish the last window sill for me, nor does he hurry off to his next client. We spend the entire day making a garden, just six feet by six, with two cherry tomato plants already bearing fruit, two of beans that are trellised, one zucchini plant, three propagating carrots, and six plants of basil which I use to border the western edge of the plot. It's beautiful. The black dirt, the green plants, even the stakes and trellises. "Is there some line about God and gardens?" I ask.

"Only God can make a tree," he replies.

"Well," I say, "this is close."

Bo tells me I need a hose, that he'll bring one tomorrow. For now, we fill and refill a bucket and drizzle water around each plant. He sings, "There's no business like grow business," and I ask him to stay for a sandwich with me. I mix up egg salad, he picks cherry tomatoes from one of the plants, and I arrange them artfully on the top of each sandwich. We pop two beers and toast to our day's work, remarking that there has never been a tomato as sweet as these little cherries he just picked in my new garden. It's a celebration. A bit of breeze stirs through from front door to back, and Bo tells me a story about the abandoned mining camp he lived in years ago on the Colorado-Utah border. There it was, vacated, just waiting for him. He paid no rent and nobody bothered him for several years. He called it the Crows' Nest.

I ask if he named it that or if the place already had that name.

He says a beat-up sign in the yard had the name scratched into the wood.

"So were there lots of crows around?"

"It was a pretty craggy place," he says, and that's all he says.

It's early evening. I realize how pleasantly tired I feel as I take our plates out to the kitchen, thinking maybe I should cut into the cantaloupe in my refrigerator. That's when I notice Bo is standing where he should have been sitting and Franny Hale is hovering in the spot I just left. She is so vague this time, ill-defined and transparent. And her transparency has color, like sky after rain, a pale and golden pink. Bo is transfixed by her. He doesn't move a muscle or look my way.

It's well and good to want to meet a ghost until it happens.

The whole room is chilled.

She stays for several minutes, the color and form beautiful in the way her cabbage roses are. I mean, it's a beauty I want to possess, contain, hang on to. She's different today. And then she's gone.

When he finally turns to me, Bo says, "She likes your garden."

Then he sits back down at the table, shoulders rounded into himself. "When I lived at the Crows' Nest, I was close to the desert around Moab. You ever been that way?" I shake my head. I have not. "It's an awesome landscape out there, worth the trip. Once I was sitting in my car at dusk watching the sun set and, for no reason, I started to shiver. We're talking August in the desert, and I was as cold as sitting outside at a hockey game. And then a shaft of white streaked across the road and evaporated."

He looks at me directly. "That's all that happened. The next day my father died 2000 miles away. I felt cold for months, wore layers of clothing, bought every Native camp blanket I could find on sale. I even went to the doctor to check my blood pressure."

I ask what he thinks happened.

"I have no explanation. Didn't then or now. This figment we just saw, the chill that came with her, it's the same. The line is thin and unpredictable. It vibrates."

I don't know what he means by the line.

"Between here and there," he says, and says nothing more. He brings the beer glasses over to me and nods and leaves. I watch from the door as he drives off in that way we watch people leave us when we are not quite ready for them to go.

The backyard is in shadow now, my garden delicate in new

dark earth. When two crows call to one another from the birch tree above, I tell them not to even consider my garden. "Do not even consider it," I call out. As if I had control of the situation.

# 33

## Like The Pale Stain From A Raspberry

"How are your roses, Floria?" Maeve asks over the phone.

"Petals to the ground, Maeve," I say. "I planted a garden yesterday, though. And Franny Hale returned all in pink."

"Well, you must get me back over there to see for myself."

When I ask, "How are you today?" she skirts it. Some topics are less interesting than others.

"Would you like to come get me now, dear?"

Today is a different day. No clouds and an entire orchestra of bird voices. I march across to Maeve's and push her gingerly over our lumpy yards to my porch, Eddie following. "Who would have thought we lived on such rocky terrain," she comments as we bump along. "You have to be old to discover the true nature of things." Even so, I see that she is pleased.

"I don't think you'll meet my ghost in the morning light," I tell her and park her chair inside the porch.

"I like being over here," she says as Eddie settles at her feet. "Your house is closer to the water than mine."

"We could go out on my dock if you want, be closer yet."

Maeve laughs. "I'm fine. I don't want to say it aloud, but I do believe my dock days are over."

"That's ridiculous," I argue. "You can still sit on a dock, feel the water underneath. Maybe see a fish."

She's staring out at the lake. "Here's what I cannot do, dear girl—I cannot take a wild leap off the end out there or row my boat to the mouth of the bay and fish by myself before the sun comes up." She keeps her gaze on the water. "Now tell me about your garden. My poor lettuce has all gone to seed."

I tell Maeve I'm surprised it has taken me so long to come

to gardening. It was such a part of my history. A constant topic of my childhood. The size of the tomatoes, how high the corn reached, berries over here, cucumbers climbing the fence, zucchini vines everywhere like weeds. And flowers planted along all sides of the house and garage, nipped and pruned and their colors orchestrated.

"Well, now you've made your ancestors proud," Maeve says.

I tell her how they are always around. "All of them, Maeve. They kind of loiter at will, give advice now and then, raise an eyebrow like you just did."

"No wonder you never remarried. You aren't lonely enough."

"I guess I'm not," I answer, and on cue, Bo Linney appears on the other side of the screen.

"Don't mean to interrupt," he says.

"No, no, no," Maeve says and introduces herself before I get to it. Bo does the same, back and forth, the two of them about the weather and my grand little porch here. Neither of them need me at all. Then Maeve says, "I came by to see her pink ghost."

"Well, she's real. I could barely sleep last night thinking that one through." Bo has come inside now and is sitting cross-legged on the floor by Eddie, rubbing the dog's ears.

"And what did you conclude?" Maeve asks.

"I didn't feel bad in her midst, I'll say that, quite a chill but a good vibe overall."

As soon as he says this, I realize that last night Franny Hale had not left me longing and restless as she always did. I share this with Maeve and Bo, this difference.

"It's your garden," Maeve says.

"That's what I said too," Bo tells her. A robin lands on the grass near the porch, skitters about searching for worms.

We are all watching the robin when Maeve says, "I would surely like to ask this pink ghost a few questions about how she manages to come and go as she does."

Bo tells Maeve that he just called out her name and she made an appearance, but I counter him. "She comes when she wants to come," I explain.

"Well, I told you that was true," Maeve says. "This ghost of yours is the one in charge. And suddenly she's pink?"

"Like my faded wallpaper," I say. "Like the pale stain from a raspberry."

"Like your bleeding hearts?" She points out several low plants on the far edge of lawn near my neighbor's woods, so tucked under other larger bushes that I had not noticed them. The tiny abundant flowers are a deep and vibrant pink.

"No," I say. "Not like that. Franny is translucent."

Bo confirms this.

"Ah," Maeve responds, as if what I said has a larger meaning. "I'd prefer to return a much deeper color, I think."

# 34

## There Will Always Be A Next Time

Bo has primed the new sills before driving off to his next appointment, but Maeve visits with me for hours. Midafternoon I make us iced coffee with sweet cream. "We need pie," she announces.

"I've never been one for pies," I say, "though my mother and grandmother were masters. When the apple trees ripened on the backyard tree, my mother would make twenty pies in an afternoon then pop them all in the freezer." I tell Maeve the story of my grandmother's banana crème pies made with seven egg yolks for the pudding filling and seven whites for the meringue.

"Now, you see," she says, looking wistful, "that is a pie."

But I have no such confection to offer.

"Do you like that man?" she asks.

"Yes, and I've agreed to be in the one-act play he wrote about Macbeth and a cleaning lady."

Maeve finds this very funny. "My husband would say 'strange the ties that bind.' This could be the start of something, Floria."

But I'm not so sure. "Companionship is one thing," I say. "Love is something else." Though the first can lead to the latter, I agree. "I'm not twenty anymore, Maeve. I like my time alone."

"By my mid-twenties I had two children and another on the way. I suppose I hardly knew what hit me. But I understand what you say. I grieved Jim terribly, I did, and then I began to find some habits of my own. Scrambled the newspaper any old way. Slept in the middle of the bed. Skipped breakfast. Stayed up into the late hours because why not? Still, life will be long if you're lucky, dear. I find this Bo to be quite interesting. A man his age who summons a pink ghost and writes about Macbeth must surely be interesting company."

"Well, he knows how to fix things," I say.

"Now you see that's a benefit too. Jim was not handy. But one of the girls has a husband who doesn't mind doing a repair here and there and I tell you it makes home ownership much easier."

"I didn't choose not to have children, you know."

She doesn't respond for a while, and no need really. We sip our iced coffees, watch the usual show out on the lake this time of day. "I didn't choose to have all my children either," she says. "Not the way you choose to buy a house or paint a wall bright yellow, you know, throw out everything you used to wear when you were thirty pounds thinner. Some things just roll along. If you'd married younger, if your husband had not died, if you'd found someone else quickly." She trails off.

"My college roommate had a poster that said *To not decide is to decide.* Some philosopher said that. It was a big idea back then."

"My generation never said such things. Took too much effort to figure them out. After the Depression and the war, nobody was in the mood for complicated notions. I think my peers were all more straightforward than yours. Don't you agree with me?"

I am remembering the time when the Catholic Church changed its Christmas wording from "peace on earth, goodwill to men" to "peace to all whom the Lord has chosen." Young, idealistic, and incensed by the overture of exclusion, I asked my parents if they didn't find that offensive, a wayward move away from peace, in fact. We'd just returned from the Mass where this new wording had been announced. My mother stood with her coat on, regarding me without comprehension and said, Oh I never listen to what he says.

So, I tell Maeve she is probably right. Her generation either chose or did not choose without attaching philosophical largeness to any of it. As she said, life rolled along. Maeve had eight children and I had none.

"I'd give him a go," she says then. "Bake him a pie or something. Right, Eddie? I'll play you two a tune to put you in the mood, get you past all the rotted window sills and whatnot. *Just tea for two and two for tea,*" she sings. "Have you heard that one?"

I tell her I have and she boasts that whenever I want to come over she'll play me her rendition. A blue heron swoops to the edge of my shoreline, a grassy area that Bo and I decided to save from his clean up. It may be the same bird that Bo spotted a week or so before, as there never are many of them.

"Why do we see so few herons, Maeve?"

"They are solitary hunters," she answers and looks my way with a kindly smile.

When I bring her home, she insists on playing me her quaint song about tea for two. Eddie is happy to find his food bowl again and one of her daughters arrives to do what daughters do. The house has most of the comfortable clutter it had when I first met Maeve, which I take as signs her life is improving again, returning to what it was before she fell and was whisked off to the hospital.

She thanks me for the nice time. "But your ghost did not come by to see me, did she?"

"Next time," I say. For, of course, there will always be a next time.

# 35

## Walk As You Must

I want to piece together Franny Hale's life with the few scraps I have of her. The paintings are dated 1903, and she was sophisticated enough to do such work, so how old would she have been then? Sixteen or seventeen, I decide, meaning she was born in 1886 or 1887. Somewhere in New York, most likely. She and John bought this cottage when it was nearly new I've been told, and I know for a fact it was built in 1902. I put weight on this certainty. If Franny and John arrived here in 1906, she would have been the same age I was when I lugged my books and typewriter from place to place looking for my own kind of adventures.

There is no way to know what she and John did from that time until he went off to World War I. What does a young couple without children do for a decade? What did my husband and I do?

Once we took a trip to Key West together. We got lost leaving the Miami airport and drove down dangerous sorts of streets before making our way back to a highway. Key West is so very far south, in the middle of the ocean really, and by the time we arrived at our bright yellow rented house, we understood ourselves to have been transported to another place. Maybe a place of Ernest Hemingway's six-toed cats and Jimmy Buffett's bar, but also a place of muted identities, of those willing to live so far on the edge they could be cut loose at any moment.

We stayed for two weeks and by the time we headed home had forgotten almost everyone we ever knew. On the flight out of Miami we sat dazed, chatted about getting a cat or taking in a stray, painting the outside of our house some shade of coral or trying to grow a lemon tree. That was one thing we did as a young married couple.

We also puttered around a lot, went to dinner a lot, saw every decent movie that showed at the neighborhood theater. Summer weekend afternoons I liked falling asleep in the backyard and my husband liked foraging for twigs and weeds and ridding us of both. We read books and chatted about people we knew and those we wished we knew. He dreamed of talking with Joseph Campbell and I with Susan Sontag, but I do not remember why. Had we known our time together would be so brief, maybe we would have done other things. I don't have an answer for that.

I imagine an early twentieth-century version of this for John and Franny: daily life, conversations, puttering along. Then the war began, he left and in 1918, when Franny was thirty-one years old, Charles came by to visit. For a few days, maybe a week, and she kept the drawings all her life because she liked her work, she liked the man, she liked remembering. But they weren't pounded into the mantel as they are now. They hid between the pages of seed catalogs, stacked in the shed out back for nearly a century.

When the war ended, John returned and within a few years they had two sons, who must have slept in the second bedroom nook here, listening to the lake at night as I do, the owls calling out, the crows complaining. There would have been mansions along this lake then and maybe the Hale property extended farther than it does now, encompassing my neighbors' land possibly and the woods and shrubs that separate me from my neighbors. I think what a grand time they must have had, a young family with two boys, living this close to the water. Frogs and worms. Fishing in a boat like Maeve's and swimming far out from shore together. Kids living on lakes don't ride their bikes around the block, but down the road, facing into the oncoming traffic, which in their age would have been just a few noisy automobiles driven by the rich and bold.

Pink wallpaper and roses aside, this had to have been a place of boyish escapades. Curious energy and experiment. John with his radios, Franny her painting and heirloom plantings, their boys following suit—building, crafting, discovering on their own. Then another war took those boys off to more serious adventures which, according to Harold, eventually led them both elsewhere. Franny and John lived alone here then for the rest of their lives.

They did not land in wheelchairs like dear Maeve, but chugged along, one decade following the next until the lakeshore became another kind of place, populated by whole new houses, split level and neo-colonial, two-story decks and four-car garages though the Hales never had even one. Staying put used to be a common thing. My parents lived on the same plot of land from the day they were married until the last one died. My grandparents as well. Feet first, they'd all say, the only way they would ever leave.

Now I want to stay too—in my cottage which would not appear to inspire permanence, its lack of a basement and the earth sinking slightly beneath it. Maybe I would have remained in my first house with my husband all these years had he lived. Or stayed in my terraced flat with its tall windows had I owned it. But those are things that didn't happen. A long story of what didn't happen, as Billy Wilder once remarked of the movie *Apollo 13*.

So Franny and John stayed even though their sons lived far away. And Franny still stays though her time has passed and her claim is illusory. I scribble all this onto paper as if to find rationality in the shape of words and dates, as if some underlying truth will emerge to explain why Franny hangs on. The researcher in me keeps asking questions while the observer in me sees Franny's life as mostly satisfying, rich even. I see no nagging reason for her to remain.

*Dear Franny*, I write, taking care with my letters so they are as clean and expressive as her own writing on the backs of her artwork. *Dear Franny—Everything I know about you tells of beauty. Even your face, which shows and fades. The full life you lived here on this lake. Is there no way to take it with you? Won't you continue forward? Find your next place, Franny,* I find myself urging. *Go on. Go on.*

I fold my scribbled notes of Franny's life and place them into a heavy book of Édouard Manet's work. This seems fitting. He was an artist not easily classified, a mystery to his peers who, besides painting dark and mythic pieces, also delighted in simple flower bouquets and the complex femininity of women's faces.

The letter to Franny I set on the table, anchored by just such a bouquet as Manet might have painted, those strands of wild-flowers which Maeve finds lovely, a few sprigs of bleeding heart in the mix. Maybe she will read it, I tell myself. Or sense it. At any rate, the letter is here for her.

It's a July day for the record and I head out for a row in Maeve's boat, ready to bounce on the wake of the powerboats or pull oars and drift if I choose.

# 36

## Trying Not To Think

Two days have passed without word from Bo. Maeve called to tell me she liked seeing me out in her rowboat. "Isn't it a fine thing?" she asked. "To be rowing along the shore of this bay?" And who could say otherwise.

I asked her about the fishing. Maybe I should take up fishing. "Oh, Floria, that's a whole other story." She laughed and I laughed back, not sure if she was in favor of my idea or not. My father always fished, I told her, it's a meditative thing. Plus the fish. But she only laughed again, then excused herself to do some-such with the attending nurse. That was Wednesday. After that, nothing.

And nothing from Franny Hale either. My note to her stays on the table, petals from the wildflower bouquet dropping onto the page, but I leave the fading flowers in their vase there anyway. I leave everything to be what it is. The garden keeps growing, a few more green tomatoes on the vine, the beginnings of beans and zucchini flowers, though all the raspberries are gone. The last few I cooked with sugar into a sort of jam that I've been spooning onto toast for two days now.

It's Saturday and I've been here five weeks. I think I've done well in my new life. I like how things are going, though these last few days I feel the absence of Bo and Maeve, wonder what they're doing. I could walk across to Maeve's on any pretext and surely be welcomed, but there are several cars in her drive always and I choose not to disturb whatever is happening there.

When I awoke this morning, it was so early, the dew remained on the grass and the lake held the silence of night, its surface glossy and still. I stood on the end of my dock surveying the water, possibly the only person out just then. There were no solitary souls fishing at dawn with hat brims pulled low and lines cast into the deeps.

And now the morning has rustled past that quiet to the full force of a summer Saturday. I watch two girls water-ski side by side, the man at the helm keeping an eye on them as he steers forward toward the mouth of the bay and into the wider lake, the girls' squeals trailing like the small waves behind them until their small neon-suited bodies round the bend out of sight. I go back into the cottage to put on my own swimsuit, dark and modest, a serious swimmer's suit, which I do not deserve but love to wear nonetheless. I slide into the water and float, squinting at the sky and trying not to think.

I have read so many books on this art of non-thinking, but they have, to a one, left me thinking more. Here and now I breathe deeply as I float, for that is another premise of not thinking. To focus on breath. To let go of everything else and only breathe. Of course, the sun is a bit too bright from where I am, so I do need to consider that and turn and paddle in a different direction. Next I drift too close to the dock and so must think about whether to let this happen or push farther away.

I continue to breathe as deeply as I know, but it doesn't stop the little thoughts that waft in and out like the cirrus clouds above me. Then a gull lands at the end of my dock and hollers my way. Is this the same gull who ate the half sandwich I left here a day or so ago? *Hello,* I call back, but I am still breathing and in my focus on the gull, I think of nothing else. I rock along on the surface of the lake and think of nothing else. All I need is the water's rhythm and one cranky gull to be a person who, for these moments, thinks of nothing else.

It might be that moments have swollen to become a whole hour and more. When my head is half under water, the noisy lake recedes to an echo, to vibrations without definition, so that by the time I wade to shore, I am somewhat dazed, almost weightless. If I am hungry, I do not know it, if chilled, abstracted, or tired, I cannot say. Inside, the clothes I pull on feel warm and the cottage smells of old wood and smoke.

It is an interlude. Something came before and more will come after. Now is this, a splendid this.

## 37

### Heads Down, Tails Up

It's midday Sunday when Bo's van finally clatters down the drive, and I know immediately he's not here to check on the garden. He's not moseying along, for one thing. Even the way his tires slide into their parking place signals an urgency. I'm in my minuscule kitchen and hear the van. I see Bo bound out and go to meet him at the back door. "Got a minute?" he calls the second I appear.

I offer him coffee, which he declines, but he comes inside to sit at my table, where he spots the letter to Franny Hale, littered now with the wilted wildflower petals. "Nice," he says after reading it. "New strategy?"

"No harm in asking her," I tell him.

"See? That's exactly what I say. I bet you've even heard me say it." Bo is wound up today. "Is it working?" he asks.

"I haven't seen her since I wrote the letter. But it's only been four days."

His head is bobbing in favor. "It's a decent request though. She probably appreciated that. *Go on, go on,*" he quotes. "That's nice."

I'm sitting across the table from him and ask what's up, this surprise Sunday visit.

"I've had an offer I can't refuse," he answers, then stops. I don't know why he stops. Has he been paid to murder me? Is he getting married? Maybe to the real estate agent with the red fingernails?

"A job."

"A building project?"

"Nope."

"You're buying a tugboat?"

"Hey, not a bad guess. I'm going back to Port Aransas, where I worked the tugs, to look after things for a friend of mine. He's taking off on a year-long trek and needs someone to run his tourist shop, sells trinkets and postcards, that kind of stuff, and I'm going to live in his house, too, and watch over the dog. He called last night." Bo is lit up like this is the opportunity of a lifetime.

"You've been to the Gulf, right?" he asks. When I nod, he says that the beaches of Port Aransas are paradise. "Clear warm water, wide sands." He kind of shivers with anticipation. "Be so nice to go back. Get that salt air into my lungs again."

"The ocean is something to miss," I say.

"That's it. I mean it's pretty here. I love these trees for sure, but where's the wonder? Where's the majesty? No mountains, no magnificent body of water, nothing here to knock you over."

I remind him of his waterfall up north.

"Exactly!" He slaps his hand on my old table. "I have to go over 200 miles north for a moment of wonder." He's calming down again and adds, "Anyway, it'll be a good year for me. I'm up for it."

"What about your play?"

"No big deal. Put it off for a year. You're still my leading lady, though, so don't run off while I'm gone."

"I don't know," I say. "Way leads onto way."

"You think I won't come back?"

"Just saying."

"Naw, that's too predictable. I basically like the gig here. It has potential, even without an ocean. Got the lake anyway. And I do love winters. I guess winters are a kind of wonder." He smooths his hair and strokes his beard. "You can come along if you want to."

"I just got here," I say, and start to laugh. "That's all I need is one more crazy move."

He wants to know if it was crazy of me to move here, his face telling me he thinks not.

“I don’t know yet,” I answer. “I pretty much walked away from a decent life.”

“But I bet you weren’t on a lake,” he responds, “or an ocean or mountain. Or by a raging river.”

I tell him that, actually, I was quite close to a somewhat raging river.

“And your name wasn’t Floria. Think you’ll ever tell me what it was?”

“I’m coming to like Floria.”

He shifts around in his chair. “Yeah, well, I can see that. I could probably use a name from an opera myself.”

“Macbeth is an operatic character.”

But this is not what he has in mind and now that his news is out and I have reacted with only polite camaraderie, he falls silent. Nods. Moves his lips in and out and picks at the flower petals on the table. Outside someone’s boat roars past close to shore.

“Sure I can’t get you anything?” I ask.

“I’m fine. I plan to finish my projects, maybe take me two weeks, wrap things up and I’m off.”

“I’ll miss seeing you,” I say, without mentioning that I miss him every time his van bumps up to the road. I don’t know why I don’t say this. I suppose it seems like unchartered water, a part of the lake I’ve not traversed and think I should not.

“Well, we’ll get together before I go. Couple of dinners? What do you think?”

I like this. “Great idea,” I say, and we decide that we’ll do a dinner on Wednesday. That’s only three days away, so we won’t have time to lose our rhythm. He’ll bring a chicken and a bottle of something good and I’ll do the rest.

He stands up and adjusts the letter to Franny Hale on the table. “Be interested to see what happens here.”

“You never know,” I say.

Before Bo leaves, he walks around the outside of the cottage to check if he’s missed any critical project that will only get worse in his absence. He thinks the back steps here need some attention, he'll get those in shape before he goes. I say thank you, he does such good work, has been so kind.

"Floria, my dear, it could be no other way," he replies, pulls himself tall and walks to his van.

I pour the rest of the coffee into a fancy cup from my mother's set. I place it on a matching saucer and walk down to sit on the dock, where I take dainty sips and consider Bo's news. It's one thing to leave, I think.

It's another to be the one who does not.

# 38

## Bananos, Bananas

Sunday evening I called Maeve, but received only her voicemail which, as usual, instructs callers not to leave a message. Several cars are in her driveway and have been all weekend, but I have seen no picnics or yard games. Two grandsons pushed off in the red rowboat, but they returned without fanfare and retied the boat to the dock.

Now, early Monday, I try her number again and get no answer. Two cars remain in the drive and some shades are drawn. The silence over there disturbs me. I have not even seen Eddie bounding about, though I suppose someone might have taken him for a walk somewhere else. When you do not know things, the suppositions can be limitless, and I want to know because Maeve is my friend. She brought me banana bread my first week here.

My mother had a lifelong friend, Grace, whom she met when they were children. My mother was small, dark, and resolute, while Grace was tall, blonde, and gregarious. I cannot remember my mother ever telling a joke, whereas almost everything Grace said struck me as funny. When I heard her voice at our door, I'd come from anywhere in the house to listen to her. She could have done stand-up comedy, I really think so. Her husband said "bananos" instead of bananas; she had a whole bit wrapped around that one fact. And her stories were always in good humor. She and my mother went to the movies together as little girls and later dancing together with their husbands. They had children close in age and started a bridge club together, shared baking recipes and gossip about the old Italians they knew around town. My mother died first and when she did, Grace told me she continued to drive by the house daily, whispering, "Hello, dear friend" as she passed.

I didn't find a truly close friend until I was ten and landed in a classroom with Jeannie Brown. She lived across the street, and though I'd seen her there, quietly playing in her yard, neither of us had ever crossed over to meet the other. Then suddenly, we were sitting in the same row at school and walking home together. Her bedroom had wallpaper much like Franny Hale's roses here, all pink on pink, the likes of which I had never seen before. My own family painted walls, there was the difference. Jeannie's father wore a suit to work, not overalls, and their house had been carpeted throughout in a plush beige rug so thick that my feet sunk into it and left footprints wherever I stepped.

Jeannie and I were both serious and well-behaved. I'd bring my clarinet to her house and set up a stand next to her piano so we could practice our lessons together. That summer, we put our dolls into the baskets of our bicycles and rode to the far edges of town to explore. But at the end of August, her father's company moved the Brown family to someplace in Ohio. For a few months, we wrote newsy letters to one another and she sent me a box of saltwater taffy, a wonder to me at the time.

After a while, our lives moved on such that communications dwindled to nothing, though sometimes in my years of travel, I wondered if I might come across a blonde woman named Jeannie and recognize in her my childhood friend. But that only happens in books and movies. Even as a skilled researcher, I am hard-pressed to find someone with such a common name who may be living anywhere in the world by now or be gone from life completely.

I had important friends in high school who scattered in all directions and kindly friends I left behind when I bought this cottage. I cannot say any is the lifelong friend Grace was to my mother. My husband and I used to speculate on this topic of lifetime alliances. He and his best buddy played catcher and first base, respectively, on an intramural college team. Then his friend went to southern California with the dream of becoming a surfer, met a beautiful girl from Australia, and was never heard from again. My husband could not reconcile this, how his pal could leave him so absolutely. I remember tossing out a pat remark that people change and life goes on. But still, he answered, who would have thought it could happen to them?

Who would have thought?

I try Maeve's number one more time and when there is no answer, I walk over and knock on the door. Eddie does not bark, Maeve is not at her window, and no one responds to my rapping. This is confounding, because there are two cars parked in the drive. Someone must be here. I circle to the front of the house where the window is open and call out "hello, hello," a few times, then "it's Floria," and "hello Maeve?" and finally, my grandmother's favorite "yoo hoo" and "yoo hoo" again.

Nothing.

I run home, put on my life vest and hurry back to Maeve's boat. If no one can hear me for whatever reason—wearing earbuds maybe, taking a shower or helping Maeve take a shower—they'll surely see me on the lake in that red boat. Maeve will wave to me from the window as she has done before and then I'll know she is fine, that she is home. And alive. I push off the dock as if I'm on a special mission, which I am in my own way. I pull on the oars with all my strength, my father's voice suggesting I take it easy, take it easy, no rush and all, but I ignore him until I am in the middle of the bay where I am certain the rowboat is visible to anyone glancing out a window on shore.

Then I pull in the oars and sit. Two motorboats pass, causing me to tilt back and forth in their wakes, but my focus remains on Maeve's gray-shingled house, where nothing seems to stir.

Of course, I am now too far away to see activity behind the windows and curse for not having the binoculars I inherited from my husband. He brought them with him to South Africa, and they were returned to me along with his luggage and all the loose possessions found in his rental car—maps, a travel guide, and a compass. How paradoxical, I thought at the time, that he'd bring a compass to keep from getting lost, then lose his whole life on a road taking him to some exact destination.

I bob about in Maeve's boat and wait. I wait for someone to come or go, for Eddie to run circles in the wide yard, for a glimpse of my friend in her window. But none of those things happen and after an hour passes, I begin to worry about the sun, for I've come out here without a hat nor any protection. Also, I am terribly thirsty. I row back slowly and pull up against her dock feeling defeated.

I try her door one more time, then go around to look at the cars parked behind the house. It crosses my mind to reach inside and lay on a horn, but the doors of both cars are locked. I trudge home the back way, through the raspberry bushes and toward my garden where the basil is full and the tomatoes all bear fruit. My beans are almost ready to pick now and the tufts of carrot greens have grown thick.

Let go of worry, I tell myself.

Plan your dinner with Bo.

Pull some weeds, my father's voice says. And so I do.

# 39

## Of Comings & Goings

My grandmother's cousin Rigio came to visit for a few days the summer I was four. He stood tall and trim and wore a dark blue suit and white shirt every day. I don't remember a tie. Perhaps he had no tie or my very young mind did not register one. Rigio's hair was white, his eyes merry. He brought me a taffeta dress from Italy trimmed with red velvet ribbon and a gathering of cherries at the waist. He also gave me a flat tin of crayons, the colors written on them in Italian.

Everything he did seemed magical, and certainly memorable, for here I am today recalling the smallest details. He smiled all the time and made my grandmother laugh. Despite the July heat, she cooked ravioli, roasted a chicken, and baked one of her specialty banana crème pies. Others in the family came to her house that week to see Rigio from Italy, who hugged each one close and laughed in greeting, all of them speaking animated Italian, words jousting into one another and rolling along for hours on end. My grandpa filled bottle after bottle of his homemade wine from the old barrels and everyone drank, even my grandmother, whose face flushed deeper with each sip.

He left late one evening after I had gone to sleep and never visited again. I don't know why. The Old Country was a mysterious place, some came from there not to return and others hopped back and forth annually, owned houses in both places and spoke comfortably in two languages. Stories traveled even more frequently back and forth. I lived in the midst of relatives I never saw, not even in photos, but I heard of their weddings, their businesses gone bad or babies growing, names of people who stayed in one village for a lifetime and names of the wanderers who rambled beyond.

I don't remember hearing about Rigio after that one visit, though I'm sure things were said. For me he lived only in those few days when I was a child and overwhelmed by his charm. I kept the tin of crayons. I'm a bit embarrassed to say I have them still, in the dresser drawer here along with the few photos and greeting cards that survived my move.

I think of him today in the context of comings and goings. It's not unnatural to gravitate from here to there. Don't the classic stories of childhood make this clear? Dangerous flights through dark and gnarly woods, journeys to the center of the earth, across the sea, the top of the mountain or even just to a different mountain than the one that is known. Governesses crossing half of England's moors to find work, and wizards passing through invisible train depot doors. When I was a child, I found a library book translated from the French about a girl named Perrine whose father died and left her alone in the world. She traveled dusty roads, set up a makeshift home on a tiny island, and ate leaves and berries until she could get a job in a factory that allowed her to buy a bit of bread and cheese. Hers was an adventure of leaving. By the end of the story, it also became a story of arriving and that is the happy part. Leaving opens the door to something else.

The wind is brisk today, the lake slapping away loud and foamy. A real lake, I tell myself, deep and active and beloved by many species. I see three gulls swoop to shore and soar away again. Off the far end of my dock, a small fish swims in a school of several others, tails in motion and eyes wide. And, of course, there are flies now, large and busy, and altogether unwelcome. These are no mere houseflies. Their bite makes that clear. Bo tells me the frogs eat them, be kind to the frogs, but truthfully, so far I have seen no frogs.

Before I met my husband, I left several men, and several left me, all mostly a blur to me now. One went to study at Oxford, another escaped back and forth to Dublin writing an Irish novel. I never left town in that way, but simply closed the door and did not open it again.

Kicking at the water, splashing idly, I look to Maeve's house. I don't know if she's there or if she too has left. Nor do I know what to make of Bo's leaving. He thinks it's all a romp, hanging out in a trinket shop near the beach for a year. Not even a real departure, he thinks. And maybe that's true. Maybe he'll be back and I'll have something new needing a fix and another garden needing his help. Maybe so.

But, as I said, I never saw my grandmother's cousin Rigio again after his one visit. Nor my husband after the airport doors closed behind him as he embarked on his adventure to South Africa.

Once people are out of sight, they are out of sight. This I've learned of leaving.

# 40

## Your Eyes Are Awfully Blue

Wednesday, promptly at six p.m., Bo peers through the screen. "French wine and free-ranging chicken, here we are!" His ponytail is tidy, his shirt pressed though hanging loose. The free-ranging chicken, already glazed and roasted, is hot and Bo carries it in a pan wrapped with a towel. When he hands me a bottle of Bordeaux with a fancy label, his eyes roll to the ceiling. "We are going to have a feast, Floria-Not-Floria."

I say he's outdone himself.

I've set the table using my mother's best bridge club cloth, embroidered with colorful sprigs of summer flowers at each corner. I've tossed a salad of tomatoes from the garden and another of noodles with vegetables and cheese. I've also baked a loaf of bread, the simple kind my mother used to make with just a bit of butter in the dough. I do not do this often and always feel her waiting for the error she is certain I will make. Not that she means to be critical, but there is a way to do things and I do tend to improvise. Still, it's a gorgeous loaf of bread, if I do say so myself.

Bo spots it immediately. "You're tempting me to stick around, is that the deal?" He leans in and takes a whiff just as my husband used to do. "But no shrine to Franny Hale on the table?"

I tell him that the note to her was finally so covered in flower petals, I brushed it clean and taped it to the refrigerator. Then I picked more wildflowers and here they are front and center on my mother's tablecloth.

"And no Franny?" No Franny, I answer. No Maeve, either, I add, and tell him about the strange silence at my neighbor's house, the lack of response to my calls. "I saw a car over there when I pulled in," Bo says, and I agree that there is always a car or two, though not always the same ones. "What about her dog?" No Eddie either.

It bothers me so much, I think if I am to enjoy my dinner with Bo, I have to stop talking about Maeve. But I do say that I'm worried. "I met her just a month ago, but she feels like someone who knows me well. And I her. It's a more immediate connection than I'm used to, I guess."

Bo listens, looks at me intently. "It's nice when that happens. Kind of out of time and space."

"It has to do with the lake, with both of us coming here for similar reasons, and loving it the same way. I mean, it's not a modern place to either of us. It's old or old-fashioned to us. Raspberry bushes and a red rowboat."

"Plus that shed," Bo says. "All that old stuff. Like I told you, almost nobody keeps that kind of junk anymore."

"Anyway, I miss seeing her." I uncork the wine, pour us each a glass, and settle into a chair that faces the mantel. Bo sits at a right angle, looking outward through the porch toward the lake and we begin to eat, more focused on the food and our respective views than on each other. At least, we don't talk just now. We eat and share the space. There is almost always a breeze coming through this room, so it's nice. Everything about the hour is nice. Bo tells a chicken story. I tell him about making bread in a family of women with an uncanny knack for baking. We hear voices across the lake, of course, brought in on the friendly breeze which seems to love us all around here, noisy or not.

When I catch Bo's eye, we both smile easily. His eyes are quite blue, I notice, but I do not say. Instead I ask who will watch over his house while he's gone. "One of the actors over at the community theater is looking for a place," he says. "So it will work out perfectly. She'll move in and hang out, pay the monthlies."

"All on a handshake?"

"All on a big bear hug," he answers. "Trust, dear woman. It's all about trust." Then he says that there's nothing of value in his house to worry about. "Love the earth but own it not," he tells me. "That's Thoreau," he adds.

"I know," I say. "Personally, I'm happy to finally own a bit of property." I'm quite emphatic and Bo laughs like I've just said something funny. But I am serious.

"Of course, I meant no offense."

"You're in adventure mode and I'm nesting," I say, thinking this sums it up.

"I never really nest," he says.

"Have you ever been married?"

He suddenly decides to arrange the silverware across the center of his plate. "Yes. I was married for three years, four months, and five days."

"And?"

"And then I wasn't."

"You don't want to tell me the story?"

I see that he prefers not to. He sighs and pours us both a bit more wine. "I like people, I really do, especially women, truth be told. But marriage did not seem a natural state of being for me."

"Well, it's a social thing," I say. "Creates stability, even safety. Most species have some kind of social order."

"Oh, sure they do. Snakes eat their mates after a good time and lions will kill pups they think belong to some other male lion. Lots of good order out there, but I don't think humans necessarily have a natural instinct to mate for life. Works for some and I'm happy as peach pie for them. But three years, four months, and five days was enough for me."

I ask again what happened and he shakes his head. "Why sully a good time?"

That's his response, but when I persist, he leans his elbows on the table and tells the story. His wife was a friend from college, an easygoing type like himself, who came from money and knew it would always be there. Which could have been true for him, too, coming from a family of bankers, but he chose not to weave his family's money into the fabric of who he was or wanted to be. He felt hopelessly attracted to her effortlessness, the way her long hair would fall out of its arrangement and she'd let it be that way. Like she hardly noticed her beauty or her potential. They had a small wedding with lots of flowers and food and music, but not much formality. No fancy dresses or tuxedos, no church candles or the like. They stood together, barefoot and holding hands. "All good," he says. "Very good."

They rented a house about the size of my cottage in a quiet neighborhood of their city, got an Irish setter and named her Lucille. Still good. He worked at this and that, she kept thinking about work but never took a job anywhere doing anything. She liked to read all day and play with Lucille. She wasn't interested in traveling because they would have to leave the dog at home. She wasn't interested in going to plays or concerts or art galleries because she'd already done too much of that in her life. Her mother had insisted on a cultural education throughout her childhood. She also chose not to cook, but nibbled around the edges of whatever he bought and put together.

She was kindly enough. Always pretty and confident and casual. But they became two people who did not move when the planet moved, who never moved at all, day after day after day.

"She wasn't ready for marriage," I say.

"She wasn't ready for life."

I ask what happened to her, but he doesn't know. He doesn't try to know. "It was a chapter," he says. "And it's over." He tells me he learned that everyone needs to be whoever they are without the expectations of a partner. "Who was I to say that she shouldn't sit like a bump on a log all the time? And who was she to say I shouldn't roam the country like a peddler?" His eyes ask a response.

"No one," I answer. "No one's to say." I counter that it may simply have been a poor match. That they were very young. Perhaps it was not enough of an experiment to toss marriage out as a reasonable idea.

"But I have," he says. "Unless you want to marry me and put my name on the deed to this place."

"You never know," I answer.

I get up, stack the dishes, and carry them into the kitchen. I hear Bo out on the front porch, whistling a show tune I cannot name. I don't want to marry him, of course. I probably don't want to marry anyone again. Still, it's not unreasonable to contemplate, is it?

# 41

## I Can Sit On This Porch Until The End

Both my husband and I resonated to oceans. I suppose that is not uncommon, though we'd fallen in love with different oceans or, I should say, different beaches. When he was a child his family rented a house in Myrtle Beach every summer, where he clambered down more than a dozen wooden steps to a wide stretch of warm white sand. He and his dad clocked the tides, charted the moon, and watched from the high and rickety front porch as storms moved in along the coast. He grew up in New York City, knew and loved the Atlantic.

My first sight of an ocean was the Gulf of Mexico. I'd traveled to Panama City for a college conference one spring, but I attended no meetings. The roar of the water pulled me toward it and I walked and walked. Naively, I even walked at night. I just couldn't stay away. Later I befriended the Pacific when my work took me to the California coast and to Seattle and Vancouver. I crossed both oceans many times.

This morning a cool wind gusts in from Canada, or so the radio announcer explains, kicking up the highest waves I've seen on this lake. I stand at the shore to be part of the ferocity and to keep watch on Maeve's boat over there bouncing and banging against the dock. I'm not sure what to do about it. Wanting to save the boat—and Maeve and Eddie, too, for that matter. Though who am I to say there is even need of saving.

I head up her deck stairs and knock on the door, catching sight of her kitchen through the window. No lights are on and the counters are ordered in that manner of things left behind for a time. After more knocking to no avail, I give up, return to my cottage, and call Maeve's phone again. Surprisingly, I do not hear her recorded voice at the other end, but that of a daughter saying I should leave a message and "one of us will get back to you soon."

So I do leave a message. Then I sit on my front porch to watch the waves and the line of foam forming at the shore. The clouds today are heavy, moody, more like a sky in late October than the middle of July. A good day for walleye fishing, my father would say, with the currents shifting so quickly. But there is no one fishing out on the bay just now, no one. No one at Maeve's. No voices coming from my neighbors on the other side either. Sitting here on my porch, I feel alone on this vast lake save for two gulls riding the gusts. There they go, dropping and gliding, barely moving a wing.

When the phone vibrates, I am startled, and for at least one second, confused, I've been in such a reverie. "Is this Floria?" It is not Maeve. It's her son Tom, whom I cannot recall. "Thank you for checking on Mother," he says, then continues to tell me they took her back to the hospital at the end of last week. "Her blood pressure was all over the place," he says, though I do not know what that might mean. She's not very mobile anymore, as he's sure I've noticed, and after several days at the hospital, the family has decided to move her to a care facility where she'll be more safe. There are other details as well. The place is located in a suburb I don't know. Eddie is with one of the sisters. Maeve has asked after me several times.

I answer that she must be missing the lake. "It's her life-blood," I say. It's none of my business, yet here I am speaking my mind. I am Maeve's advocate now, who else will voice what she needs the most? Not safety, in my opinion.

The silence that follows is awkward until I ask, "What does Maeve say?"

He hesitates. "She says what you've just said. She wants to be back at the house and she wants Eddie with her. But being in the house wasn't working. Even with all the help, she fell again, she wasn't eating properly, she was not doing well at all." He trails off.

"And now she's improving? She's doing better now?"

He says, "No, she is not. She's worse."

"If it were me," I say, "I would want to be getting worse in my own house with my own dog and the lake breeze coming in the window. I'm sorry," I add. "She would want me to say that to you."

"I know, I know," he answers. There is more silence and then his voice shifts, some confidence renewed, he takes a buck-up sort of tone and ends the call by telling me he appreciates my input. "I'll keep in touch," he says, and I thank him.

It was not my place to say what I said. I am nobody to this family, a new neighbor who came out of nowhere and is now behaving as if I know Maeve better than they do. They are on the brink of losing their last parent and I understand how they want to keep her alive at all costs. Take her to the hospital. Bring in any number of nurses. Cart her back to the hospital and off to a care facility. Send Eddie to live with someone else in the family, poor Eddie. How can he understand human reasoning? He knows only that he is not with the companion he is meant to protect and serve. I don't know which predicament is worse.

The wind has not diminished. In fact, its rage is near deafening and I am now back on my screened porch to witness nature's fury. Six gulls soar high, calling and crying out to one another. I watch as one dives down into the water for a fish and the others circle in what looks like a version of joy to me.

I take in the cool air deeply, the scent of the lake, its weeds and fish and the gasoline of boats.

If I ail in years to come, I will have no offspring deciding what to do about me. Like Franny Hale I can remain here. I can sit on this porch until the end, breathing in all this as I do now.

Until I do not.

# 42

## Beginnings Of A Voice

Late afternoon Bo comes by with some planks to fix my back steps. When he hollers to me, the wind scatters whatever he says like little nothings.

"What?" I yell back.

He tries again then walks to the porch door, lets himself in, and pushes the hair from his face. "Jesus, what a gale."

"We're trying to convince you of the awe that surrounds us," I say. "So you don't have to go all the way to the Gulf of Mexico for a bit of wonder."

"I guess. Whew." He sinks down into the chair next to me. That's when he tells me he's brought supplies for the steps and will be here Saturday to do the work. "We could get a pizza afterward," he says. "That place in town does the wood-fire thing. Thin crusts. Good stuff." We make a plan and sit together watching the waves crash onto shore and a single gull floating out there on the wind.

"Maeve's kids sent her off to a care facility of some kind."

"For good?"

"Sounds like. I called and one of her sons called me back. I can't imagine it, can you?"

"You mean being moved around?"

I don't think that's what I mean. "The separation," I say. "No lake, no Eddie, no familiar bed or birds outside the window. No home. No more home."

Bo rubs his forehead. "She's got her kids though."

I admit that love is something, too, but this thought does nothing to lift my heart. "I told her son to consider bringing her back here." The gull has drifted away from this side of the shore to become a far speck over the center of the bay.

Bo asks if I'll go visit her.

I hate this question. What good am I without the lake as my backdrop, without a dog at our feet or raspberries from our mutual bushes, the promise of the sun's reflection on water, a storm edging in at night? What good am I with my pretend name and no cure for anything? "I'll get the address," I say. "I'll bring her a couple of tomatoes and some wildflowers." But I announce this without conviction.

Bo thinks it's a good idea, pats my knee like some wise old uncle and tells me he'll see me Saturday. He blows past the screened windows to his van parked in the back, the loose hairs of his ponytail in mad array.

It is beginning to get dark, so I hook the screen door and turn on a lamp by the fireplace. I close the windows of the two tiny bedrooms and survey their order and charm. I am so grateful for this home.

Let me stay forever. I say this to whatever god may be listening. Let me stay. There is no heavenly response, of course, but as I move into the main room of the cottage again, I see Franny Hale, back from weeks of absence. I had thought I might not see her again, that my plea for her to go had registered. Yet here she is, the faintest image of herself now, without definition. Only a sense of Franny, a fading sunset of Franny.

I do not move and neither does she.

A lone gull, maybe the one I watched or maybe another, squawks near shore, its voice traveling from my porch into the room where Franny and I stay suspended. And then she dissolves.

I, on the other hand, do not budge for whole large minutes, swollen and heavy moments of time, and when I realize my feet are moving, they carry me to Franny's paintings on the wall: the sailboat, the tiny figure on the beach, the house on a far cliff. I have always thought of these images as the essence of departure, of leaving and not looking back. Off to sea. Far on a beach. Away from home.

Today I think the opposite. The paintings that Franny kept here all her life and which I choose to keep as well, tell stories of arriving, of returning. The boat that sails to shore, the walker heading home. And home a bright red spot in the distance.

# 43

## And Time Yet For A Hundred Indecisions

I grew up with immigrants. They were my grandparents, their friends, and their cousins. They were the shopkeepers and plumbers and builders, hairdressers and tailors and waiters in restaurants. The immigrants of my childhood came from Northern Europe, Eastern and Southern Europe, from countries of destination and small places of less appeal, and later in my life I met those from Russia, China, and many parts of Africa. They always claimed the place they left, but none had much interest in talking about why they left or when they left or even that they did leave.

They were here and that was what mattered. That was the story unfolding. They had plans, were making things happen or would make things happen soon. Maybe they already had found the dream, a house on a tree-lined street, a car and garage, kids going to school. Maybe they had money in the bank and moved through their lives like Franny did, one morning to the next, one season to the next, measured and fruitful.

Franny may not have immigrated to this country, but she traveled halfway across it to be right here, where she stayed—and seemingly remains. Why I am thinking these things, I cannot sort. Because Franny returned so quietly to me, so barely there, her image pale in comparison to other visits, I wonder if I am losing her or if this apparition is losing me. Arriving somewhere else.

The phone is a shock in all this musing.

"Floria, is it you?" Maeve booms at me.

"It's me, I'm here, so good to hear your voice again," I say.

"I'm not dying, you know."

"Of course not, of course not."

"Floria?" Her voice is even louder.

"Yes, I'm here Maeve. Are you coming back? Will you be coming home?" I'm now shouting too.

"It's a mess. Just impossible, this place has nothing to do with me. It's impossible." Her voice is modulating so she sounds like herself again, though a very tired version. "I don't seem to have much balance. That's the problem everyone says. If I'm alone, I'll fall, but honestly, Floria, falling isn't everything. Falling isn't everything. If I stay here, how will I live?"

This would be my question too, surely, but before I can fabricate a response, Maeve says, "I'm going to plot my way out, wait and see. Did you ever tell your parents they were not the boss of you, Floria? When you were a child?"

I say I don't remember ever telling them that though I thought it, as every child does somewhere along the way.

"You see now how it's all turned around? No one here is the boss of me, that's what I woke up thinking this morning. And how on earth will Eddie live without me? That is another thought I am having. So I've called to say look for me soon and not to worry. Because it is only July and there's still time." I am supposing she means there is still time for summer and the open water. Windows wide and the grass green.

"Have you picked any blueberries yet?" she asks. "Now is the time, Floria. You can find them near the lake if you look, you'll find them." Her voice trails off, she coughs, hollers, "Now is the time, Floria," and disconnects. The silence after this conversation is larger than the entire lake outside my window. I sit for the next hour waiting to hear from her again or from someone else in her life who will share a plan, tell me Mother will be home tomorrow or Sunday or a week from Sunday. But nobody calls.

The sky opens to a solid wash of blue, a different blue than winter skies. Much deeper in color and lower, as if I could reach out and seize its depths.

I put on my swimsuit, wade into the water, swim in my

haphazard fashion to Maeve's dock, rest, swim back, rest, and swim back again until I am too exhausted to wonder about her destiny or my own. I stretch a towel onto my sweet-smelling cedar dock and close my eyes. I imagine blueberries, bowls and buckets of blueberries. There is a kindly breeze today and the water rocks beneath me. *Now is the time*, Maeve said.

I drift on that and only that.

# 44

## And Take Upon's The Mystery Of Things

I am hauling the mower out of my shed when Bo shows up Saturday, but I stop to tell him everything that has happened. I explain Franny's pale presence, my pondering over leaving and arriving, the timing of things, Maeve telling me this is the time, there is still time. "As you said last week, Bo, the line is thin and wavering."

"Is that what I said?"

"Something like that," I answer. "The streak of light in the desert, your father dying. Remember?"

He's standing still before me, tool bag in hand, looking as though he sprung up out of the ground. "I have my profound moments," he says. "So the ghost came back, eh?"

"I may not see her again."

He asks why I say this and I tell him I sense it. She's a weaker strain of herself. I believe she's giving in to destiny after all these years. I tell Bo I think she's ready to arrive somewhere else, go on, as my note asked her to do. Then I follow him to my splintering back steps where we both sit.

"Garden really looks good," he says.

I thank him. I may not have done it without him and now here is all this beautiful stuff reaching and tumbling about before us. "You can smell the basil from here," I say and inhale deeply.

"You know with this Franny Hale, look what you've done for her. You dug her drawings out of the shed, pounded them into the mantel. The garden here. A beautiful new dock." He nudges me with his elbow. "Fresh paint. Windows fixed. Maybe that's the thing, just bringing her old home back to life so she can move along. Let the dead be dead, as the poem goes."

It's a reasonable conjecture, one I consider, even rather love. That I have made a ghost happy, or at least content enough to find her next place in the far, unfathomable universe.

The afternoon goes well. The sun remains high, the air easy. As I mow, I hear teenagers squealing, one boat following the next out on the water and my neighbors to the south celebrating outside with resounding bouts of laughter. An hour later Bo heads out for pizza and when he comes back, he has the inside scoop on where we can find blueberries.

We eat and plot, drink several beers, tell more stories. He kept tarantulas as pets when he was in college, shocked to find the small one half-digested in the larger one's mouth one day. "I should have paid attention," he says, finishing the last bite of crust. "But I got married the next year anyway."

I tell him about characters I've met along the way and he does the same. We're at a time in our lives where there is no end to the stories and it's good to roll them out into the open, see what there is to see. He once watched President Nixon eating in the back booth of a Los Angeles steak house. I once saw Woody Allen rushing down Fifth Avenue in New York, clarinet case in tow. "What happened to your dog Lucille?" I ask him.

He says she stayed with his wife. "They were the real team, the two of them, napping all the time."

He never had another dog. He had a few cats over the years, or they had him, found him, wandered into his life and stayed. But he has no cats now. "You should get a cat," he tells me, and I answer that Maeve thinks I should have a dog.

"Well, we all have our ideas," he replies.

It crosses my mind that he could spend the night with me. We could rollick along for a few more hours into the night and I think it would be fine and fun. We wouldn't lose anything. But we're on such a smooth playing field right now. He'll be leaving in a week. Why would I want to miss him any more than I know I will already? These thoughts bounce around in my mind as we share a last beer for the road.

By the time Bo stands and stretches, ready to go, the sun is long gone and the lake mostly hushed. One light is on in the cottage and shadows flicker. "I'll come get you tomorrow to pick some berries," he says and bows deeply from the waist, smiling such that I understand he has his thoughts too.

See you then, he calls.

His van grinds its way up the hill as one late and wayward firecracker goes off in the bay.

# 45

## Never Underestimate A Guy With A Ponytail

Many things have happened since I rode with Bo in his rattletrap van to a field of blueberries. We filled two buckets and popped nearly another bucket into our mouths and, afterward, I went home to make sweet preserves. That was Sunday. Two days ago.

When Bo dropped me off, we planned to reconvene later, he was concocting a soup and I was to throw together a salad from our burgeoning garden. As the berries foamed in the pot, the wind started to shake my screens and the sky grew dark. Weather strikes more suddenly on the lake, it seems, though maybe I imagine this. Maybe it is just that I am vulnerable to the vagaries of weather here, its outbursts and mood swings. The edges of Franny's drawings on the mantel lifted as blustery air pushed through my cottage and I scrambled to close windows. But the wind had a voice anyway, near howling as trees bent to its will and the lake rose and crashed onto shore.

Then a storm warning blared across the water, and I turned on my radio and a lamp, keeping one eye on the simmering jam and one eye on the trees surrounding me. It's not that I expected a pine to topple my way, but I stayed vigilant nonetheless. The rain came, hard and fast and slanted north to south, sheets of water pummeling the old chairs in my screened porch. When the radio announcer urged listeners to take shelter in the basement, which I do not have, or a storm shelter, which I also do not have, I sat on the floor near the fireplace and out of direct line of any window, counting by fives to calm my nerves the way I did when I was a child playing hide and seek. I heard my father reassuring me, my mother and grandmother saying no such thing, and finally, after an exhausting surge, the rain stopped and the trees sighed. I swear I heard them.

That was the first thing that happened.

Next Bo called to tell me he wasn't coming for dinner. His neighbor's tree had uprooted in the storm and landed across the front of Bo's yard. Now he needed to help clear it. He hadn't made the soup. He was sorry.

"I didn't know you had my phone number," I said, and he answered that he had his ways.

"Never underestimate a guy with a ponytail." Then he told me he wouldn't be by on Monday either as he had a project he needed to finish.

I asked when he was leaving for Texas.

"Soon," he said. But he didn't say how soon was soon.

I made a salad for myself, ate toast with warm blueberry jam, and mopped up the water on my porch floor. The evening remained so dark that I could not discern the sunset, and I fell asleep listening to the lake and the rainwater dripping off the trees. That took care of Sunday.

Monday morning Maeve's son Jimmy was out in her yard picking up a few branches that had blown in. "Hey," I called, startling him as I came his way. "How's Maeve?"

He told me she was stable.

I didn't say his mother was plotting to return to her house. Instead I asked if he thought she'd be back.

"Suppose we should bring her for a visit," he said, his eyes scanning the yard for debris rather than meeting my own. I offered to help any way I could, asked after Eddie, lingered. But Jimmy had his mind on something other than our conversation. At last, he smiled a hey-ho smile, raised his eyebrows in farewell, and left.

I did not leave when he did. I stood in Maeve's front yard in something of a trance. All the grass, the leaves on the trees, and the shrubs encircling her house shimmered in the aftermath of rain. The lake, refreshed by Sunday's downpour, lapped its quiet rhythm, and I stayed amidst all that, watching the bay, watching a duck far from shore, watching.

Monday, too, passed. The porch aired dry. I made a blueberry pie, not my mother's standard but decent enough, and managed to fit it into my tiny freezer for whenever Maeve comes to visit. Because I believe she will come to visit. Her will to return is powerful, and her children's will to resist her is hesitant. They love her and know she is unhappy. And so I look ahead to the moment when I will surprise Maeve with a pie I've made for her. Later, I took out the rowboat, came back and swam a bit, and moseyed through the hours as one does when knowing nothing large is about to happen.

Now it is Tuesday, almost the end of July. I am hoping to hear from Bo, but when my phone buzzes, it is my brother's name that pops onto the screen. I haven't talked to him since Mother's Day, when we tend to check in to review our past some and laugh at family dynamics that only we can know. "How you been?" he shouts like Maeve does, a habit he has of pretending we don't need phones to talk across country. I pour a cup of coffee and settle in one of the old chairs on my porch. "I'm fine," I say, and at that moment a speedboat zips across the bay.

My brother asks if he's hearing a boat.

"A boat it is," I say.

"So you on vacation?"

"I'm taking some time," I answer. "It's nice to be by the water."

"We're in a drought out here," he says, which I know from the news.

I tell him that Sunday night we had one of those storms where the water comes at you sideways, and this somehow brings us to the memory of the wide front porch on our childhood home. It wasn't screened, but so expansive that we could sit close to the wall of the house and be safe from the weather. Turns out we have lots of stories about that porch, a place shaded by mountain ash trees on either side of the sidewalk and those trees planted all around with my mother's orange and yellow nasturtiums. He tells me his stories, I tell him mine. We haven't talked about that porch before. The sidewalk led to an ironwork fence and gate, painted a shiny silver that my father touched up with great regularity.

"Remember trying to trim the grass under that fence?" my brother says.

"Remember pulling your books up into the ash tree to read?" I add. "And the year of the armyworms?"

"I don't remember the armyworms."

"I climbed to the top of one of the ash trees before I realized it was covered in worms. I can't believe you'd forget that."

"I wasn't the one climbing the tree," he says. "You know I think I can hear the lake water on your end."

"It's a nice sound. Rocks me to sleep and calms me all day."

"That's what I need. I need lake water lapping."

We talk for a few minutes more, back and forth about his children mostly and a few comments about the lousy politics. I am tempted to tell him that I've moved onto this lake for good, have paused my work, do almost nothing all day, am living with a ghost and growing a garden. I do not because it would be a long conversation and, at some level, my brother would not believe me. He's very solid, very practical. You don't get where you're going by lolling about on a lake forever. Though that is somewhat the point.

There is nowhere else I want to go.

# 46

## How Soon Is Soon?

Bo is not so cheerful today. A final project is spiraling into something more than what he has the time to do if he is to leave soon. Again, I ask how soon is soon and he says he hopes to be on the road by the first of August.

"That's a week away."

"Exactly." He's not looking at me but leveling the steps, concentrating, sweat all over his face in the midday sun. I don't have a response to this news, although it makes sense. It's already been nearly two weeks since he announced his grand adventure. And haven't we had our times together? And over the next week might we not have more?

"Did you ever make that soup?" I ask.

"I did not make the soup and I did not start to pack." He glances up. "I mean does a deck with a railing need a gate? Does the deck gate need a matching garden gate? Honest to god, these people do not have enough to do but think up useless add-ons to their million-dollar properties. I can hardly wait for Port Aransas where all I have to do is sell seashell keychains."

I mumble an acquiescence and disappear into the garden to see what's ripening, pinch wandering tendrils, and pretend I know what I am doing, though I am sure my Italian grandparents are dismayed. Who would let tomatoes grow undisciplined in this way? I notice zucchinis ready to pick and decide I should be the one to make the soup for Bo and me.

I holler out to him and see his distress at this suggestion. He's trying to finish my steps in a professional manner then get back to building a deck gate he finds ridiculous. The day has only so many hours and a man can work only so fast. "You want any help?" I ask. But he doesn't hear me. Or chooses not to hear me.

Coming into my kitchen, I wonder what I was thinking venturing out like I've done, assuming a cottage on a lake would be enough, that just being near water would be enough. That trees and books and a dock would suffice. Was I mad? In a moment's worry, I call Maeve, amazed that she actually answers.

"Floria," she shouts to outwit her hearing aid. "Is that you, Floria?"

We bumble around like this until she gets the sound right. Then I say, "Maeve, when are you planning to come back to your house? It is not the same here without you. I'd be happy to visit every day, do things that need to be done. Dishes or dusting, really anything."

"Isn't that nice," she says. "How is the lake out there today, Floria?"

I tell her it's still, there's hardly a ripple, the sky is hazy. "Fires out West," I say.

"You know I have a neighbor down the hall here who is a marvelous painter. She does landscapes like the ones you have hanging. A lovely woman," she adds. "You'll have to stop by and meet her." I am about to say I will try to do that, of course I'll do that, but our call is cut off. I wait a few minutes, try Maeve again, and get only her voicemail.

Maeve has made a lovely new friend. She is not talking of escaping from the place she found impossible a week ago.

Concocting my soup, I think about how easy it was to meet Maeve and Bo, who both just showed up. One at the front door with her dog and one at the back door with his old van. It isn't always that way. It's almost never that way. I lived in my high-ceilinged flat all those years and only one neighbor rapped on my door. We'd said hello, coming and going, and then, out of the blue, she stopped by to tell me the building caretaker bailed and a new one was stepping in to take his place.

I don't remember why she felt compelled to go door-to-door with this announcement, and after that we resumed our limited cordial greetings. People rented in that building and, even if they stayed for many years like I did, they possibly thought departure was imminent. At any rate, nobody brought banana bread.

My mother was the sort to bring banana bread. She made a lifestyle out of good deeds, baked for whomever she thought needed something sweet, drove her friends to the grocery store if they did not drive, crocheted blankets for every baby born to anyone she knew. After she died I heard about her kindness to friends and neighbors, her smile at the door asking nothing in exchange. It was her purpose in life, that kindness. My father did his version as well, fixing lamps for widows free of charge. Bringing packets of freshly caught fish to this one or that.

The soup has come together, salt and pepper correcting all errors, but I don't set the table. I clean a jar, fill it with some of my soup, and walk to the back door to tell Bo he can have it when he goes home. "Gave up on dinner with me, eh?" He stands and surveys the steps. "Done. One project down and two to go." He sounds very satisfied, grins, takes a deep breath.

I tell him they look perfect and this is true. They are as solid and safe as is Bo himself. I tell him he is still invited to dinner, but that I sense he needs to keep moving.

"That is because you are wise and sensible. I want all clients to be like Floria Whoever. Reasonable types, that's what I want." Bo then says I should save the soup and he'll come Friday night. All work and no play, he recites, and tells me he should be done with the gate fanatics by then. Plus, he has wine to share and cheese that won't last long on the road.

"Sounds good," I say, and it does sound good. But today is Wednesday. Two days until Friday.

"I'd recommend sealing the wood here," he adds as he packs up the van. "Harold will have what you need. Ask for a stain-sealant combo." Then he rattles off, leaving me in his dust, so to speak. Soon he will be on to his next episode. Like Maeve appears to be on to hers. It's even possible that Franny Hale has found her hereafter at last, though that is less certain.

Buddhists believe when they die, they may be reborn to another earthly life. Sometimes this happens immediately. Sometimes it takes forty-nine days. I've always appreciated that specificity. Forty-nine days is not a very long time. I've taken trips longer. I've been here in my cottage longer. Trying to imagine scuttling off to a new reality so quickly, I feel more sympathetic to Franny, bless her, resisting rebirth for more than forty years. Obviously, she was not a Buddhist. Which gets me to wondering what a Buddhist might think of Franny's ghost holding on for so long. What would be the explanation? She might be a mother of two different sons by now. Have another whole life on a lake or an ocean or a winding river on another continent. Maybe closer to heaven than she was here next to this lake.

Though, honestly, it's hard to imagine that could ever be true.

# 47

## Before The End

Before I've crossed the threshold into his store, Harold is waving to me. "Hey, I've got something for you," he calls and takes out his wallet, flips through things. "Wait a minute, it's here somewhere." His fingers pinch a small photo which he hands across the counter. Then he watches me take it in. The colors are fading on a tall teenage boy. He stands next to an elderly woman holding a magnificently oversized zucchini. Behind them, my cottage, already slightly sunk into the earth on that south side of the lawn.

Harold asks if I can tell it's him, he was fifteen when the photo was taken. But I barely hear him. I am looking at a ghost when she was alive and squinting into an afternoon sun. Oddly the person she was in the photo seems to be the ghost. This picture is someone back from the dead, showing off her gigantic garden vegetable. Harold wants to know what I need today. A customer beside me asks where to find the superglue. The bell over the door jangles and jangles again.

Clutching the photo, I say that I need to stain and seal the wooden steps leading to my back door and Harold comes away from his perch behind the counter, jokes with the superglue customer, returns with a can of wood finish and hefts it onto the counter. "There you be," he says and continues chatting as though the photo he's shown me is no more than a funny snapshot of days gone by. "Keep it," he says. "My kids were rummaging through old albums and found more of this kind of stuff than anyone needs, believe me. So you keep that one."

I pay for the sealant, thank him for the photo, and rather stumble out the door where the afternoon sun hits me with a blast of light. Was it dark in the store, I wonder, for this light to surprise me so? I'm gripping the handle of the sealant can with one hand and holding the small photo with the other, feeling clumsy and alone on the sidewalk in this perfectly ordinary small town. Walking to my car, I spot a drugstore on the corner, and make my way there, not seeing who passes me on the sidewalk, not even seeing the sidewalk. The drugstore, unlike the hardware store, is all white light, white merchandise racks, and white linoleum. I find the aisle with household decorations, fake flower arrangements and vases shaped to resemble tree trunks and plant stalks. I can't imagine who chooses such things. I am looking for a small frame for Harold's photo and here it is, pretend silver made to look like it's from another century, when frames were ornate with floral detail. It's on sale and I buy it quickly, do not want it in a plastic bag, do not want to be in the store any longer than necessary.

I want to be home with this picture of Franny Hale on the side of her house, now my house. I want to study it precisely and this I do. Before I set the photo into its cheap frame, I lay it on my table and follow every detail. Given Franny's size compared to Harold's, I place her at five-foot-two or three, no more. She is small boned and wearing loose clothing, a pair of dark pants, maybe blue or charcoal, and a flower-printed blouse tucked into the pants. It's almost a dressy blouse, faded red in the picture with a rounded collar edged in white. And the buttons are white. Her sleeves are rolled and she wears no jewelry other than a wedding band on her left hand. No earrings or necklace, not even a tiny cross like both my mother and grandmother always wore.

Behind Franny and Harold, the south side of the house shows its two narrow bedroom windows, both with crisscross curtains that were no longer here when I came along. The grass looks healthy, maybe even a bit too long by my family's standards. I sense my father's disapproval.

The photo has a faded border and on that border, 1975, printed in tiny numbers. I have to think about that date. Then I remember Harold saying it was the year Franny died, in the fall, putting her garden to rest. This picture of her with Harold may be the last taken of her, yet who would know—she stands so straight and loose, her smile unguarded, humor in her eyes, she appears as someone busy and active and something else. Pleased. Incredibly, if it can be believed, she is wearing the boots I saw her in last month, then pale and fading, here in the photo a bit heavy, almost industrial, holding her so well, as sturdy looking as fifteen-year-old Harold next to her.

I put Franny's photo into the frame carefully, relieved that I do not have to trim any of the border away to make it fit. I set it on the mantel near her drawings of Charles, pour myself a glass of wine, and listen to the faint rustle of the leaves all around this cottage. There are many things to try in life. I've traveled, walked miles, seen oceans and cities from the windows of airplanes both ascending into the sky and heavily descending out of it. I've swam and paddled, baked and now gardened, read and read and read. My mother tried to teach me to embroider, my grandmother tried to teach me to knit, my father tried to teach me to pound a straight nail, and if none of this came to fruition, it wasn't for their lack of effort. My failures may have had something to do with their lack of patience, but I don't want to dwell on that. They would surely surround me in denial, so what is the point?

The point is, I have more to do. That is the point. Standing in the middle of my cottage, glass in hand and eyes wandering, I see what I see—Franny's paintings with their dabs of dazzling red, the soft, pale sketches of Charles, the low blue summer sky reflected in the lake beyond my porch door, pink wallpaper, tiny orange tomatoes in sprigs on the counter, my grandmother's bleached white sheets. I am breathing in color, in texture, in the life of things that have been created one way or another. Whatever happens next, it has to do with all this.

Within the hour, Bo comes for dinner, and I summarize my thoughts as we wait for the soup to heat. He's slicing off chunks of the cheese he brought, taking full gulps of wine as if it were beer. It's been a long day for him, but now he's done with his projects completely. His long legs stretch out in front of him as he listens to me. "You ever think about painting?"

I have not. I fear it falls into the category with my mother's embroidery and my grandmother's knitting, something beyond my abilities. I tell him this, but he waves it off. "You did a garden," he says. "That was then, this is now, as the phrase goes. Take a class or just mess around, see what happens."

It's a nice thought, perhaps not exactly what I meant by having more yet to do in my life, but it wouldn't hurt to mess around, as he said, and see what happens.

"This whole place, this light, it's an artist's dream," Bo says, then pours more wine before adding, "You can come paint in Port Aransas, too, you know. That's another kind of light."

I thank him for his invitation, but I don't take it seriously. Bo speaks in the moment—be part of my play, jump off the dock with your clothes on, come to Texas with me, paint pretty pictures in the winter light. He's lived in an abandoned mining shack and blown about in life like the last leaf of autumn. Why would I take him seriously?

Nonetheless, I tell him, yes, I will consider painting. "Maybe by the time you return next spring, I'll have some inspired abstract for you to hang on your wall."

"Think big," he says.

We eat in near silence, but it's not uncomfortable. We are like people who have been through something significant together though all we've shared really is the building of a dock, the planting of a garden, and a few casual meals. I don't know why we have this solid kind of kinship. Now and then I catch him glancing up at the mantel to the tiny photo of Franny and Harold and when he does, I can almost see his mind at work. "What?" I ask finally.

"Kind of wild that you'd have her photo up there, isn't it? I mean, that Harold would find a photo of this woman who's been haunting your place all summer and you'd put it up there on the mantel."

"You think it's inappropriate?"

He leans on the table to look more closely at the picture. "I'm not saying that. It's uncanny, that's all. I don't know if it's a good idea to have her up there."

"Why? You think she won't like it?"

He squirms in his chair, drinks some wine, smooths his hair as he does. "I don't know. Forget it."

"I like that picture. I like how she faces into the camera. It's hopeful to me."

Now Bo regards me instead of the photo. "I thought you wanted her gone."

"I do. I want her ghost gone, but I like the way she looks in the photo." I shrug. "I think she's moved on anyway," I add. And that's where we leave it. Bo brought cookies from the same bakery that makes the best donut holes in the county and so we munch on those and keep drinking wine. Bo tells me the last awful story of his deck gate and soon there is nothing left of food or wine and it has become dark outside. He still needs to pack, has so much to do. But he tells me he will come by before he heads out of town.

"You aren't rid of me yet, dear Floria," he says and touches my face. At the door, he turns again and asks, "Will you ever tell me your real name?"

But he doesn't wait for an answer.

# 48

## Of Marvels And Happenstance

It's Saturday, the last of July, eighty-eight degrees with considerable humidity. Seventy percent, my weather app tells me. The lake is raucous with noise and movement both in and out of the bay and there is not a cloud in the summer blue sky. I drink coffee sitting on my dock and get lost in the commotion. I've never been on water skis, so the physics of this activity fascinates me. I've heard it's like riding a bike, finding your balance and holding on to it. Something you never forget how to do. Still I wonder.

Next summer, I decide, I am going to get a canoe or kayak, something not too difficult to store. When Bo returns, if Bo returns, maybe he'll build me a rack and I can begin to accumulate the things that lake dwellers have. Maybe next summer I'll look like I belong, become part of the beachy pulse, one of the casual and carefree, a new persona for me. Maybe I'll wear a ponytail like the young woman who paddles by every Sunday.

I do not see Maeve's entourage arrive and because I am at the end of my dock, I do not hear them either. They are a jolly family, as I've said, but today they congregate on her lawn as a more wobbly and unsure group. Maeve's son Jimmy pushes her wheelchair, a daughter whose name I do not remember is there and two girls in the awkwardness of late childhood. I'm not sure how long they've gathered before Eddie barks to alert me then tears across the yard to herd me into the fold. Maeve once told me she's sure he's part border collie. She waves, not half-heartedly, but low and weak. She's sunk so far down into that wheelchair, she looks half her size and as I approach, I see that she has lost weight in the short time since our last visit.

"We thought we'd have lunch lakeside," Maeve's daughter says. The two girls are laying out a quilt across the grass and unpacking plastic containers of homemade food. Jimmy stays behind Maeve's chair, holding on to it. I notice him eyeing the grass which has become longer than usual in the family's absence, but he says nothing, seems to avoid connecting with any of us.

Maeve comments on how happy Eddie is to be back and I say I'm happy to have them both back.

"It's just a picnic," Maeve's daughter says to signal Maeve is visiting, not returning. I wish I could remember this daughter's name, but cannot pull it up in my memory and choose not to ask. She invites me to join their lunch and I sit on the far end of the quilt next to Maeve's chair. I see that her hands and arms are dotted with purple blotches she didn't have before.

"Isn't it all so lovely," Maeve says, smiling in her gracious way, surveying the lake and all its to-do. The two girls hand out tuna salad sandwiches cut into triangles which they have placed carefully on thin paper napkins, though they eat theirs hopping about on the grass. One of them is trying to perfect her cartwheel, the other critiques her progress and their mother, Maeve's daughter, watches them without comment.

Jimmy does not leave his post behind the wheelchair and eats with one hand, a glob of mayonnaise dripping onto the ground at his feet. "Shoot," he mutters, and steps back from Maeve a bit so he won't drip anything onto her.

In almost every encounter I've ever had with Maeve Murphy, she has made something happen. She has that kind of energy, that kind of spark, a mind that travels randomly from one interesting nook to the next, remembering and assessing, playing a tune or asking a question. Now we all sit quietly. Nothing happens. Boats roar out of the bay, kids squeal a short way down the shore and Maeve's granddaughters go from cartwheels to attempted handstands, finally collapsing on the quilt to fiddle with each other's hair.

At least half an hour passes in this way. I find a stick and toss it about for Eddie and see Maeve smiling as the two of us play. "Did you know Floria was named after an opera character?" she announces out of the blue. "I now have one regret in life and that is I did not name any of my children after opera characters." Maeve's son and daughter seem not to be listening. Then she startles all of us by saying, "Floria, do you think Eddie could live with you?"

Jimmy starts to say something but his sister interrupts, "That's kind of a sudden decision, Mother. The girls are enjoying Eddie at home." I see she wants me to decline gracefully and let things go on however they have been for the past few weeks. But I do not do this. I reach out for Maeve's hand and grin.

"Is that what you want?" I ask. "I would love to have Eddie. For a visit," I add, making eye contact with the two girls. "You want to visit too?" I blurt this without a moment's serious thought, but the girls leap from the quilt in what I would call glee. They are crazy about this idea of visiting their grandmother's neighbor with Eddie.

"Can we stay overnight too?" That's the next theme, all bedlam with Maeve observing in a state of delight. They discuss if the girls should stay in Maeve's house with their mother, but decide it won't work, the mother has obligations, the girls' father would not approve and so on, and Jimmy puts the brake on the wheelchair and excuses himself finally to mow the lawn like any self-respecting male in these circumstances would do.

In the end, it is agreed that Eddie and the girls will come next week, the girls for an overnight and Eddie for a longer, unspecified length of time. Then the remainder of the picnic is packed up, the quilt folded, and the lawn mowed. Somewhere in there, Maeve dozed in her chair and I gave the two girls a tour of my cottage. We discussed them both sleeping together in the second bedroom on the narrow daybed I keep there. They wandered my small rooms as if in a dollhouse, touching the edges of the furniture almost lovingly and sighing over details like the drawings of Charles pounded into the mantel and the little kitchen with ripe tomatoes in a bowl. I tell them the cottage is more than a hundred years old and the younger of the two gasps. "I can't believe we get to stay here," she says.

Just before they leave, Maeve and I find a moment when nobody else is near. "Do you hear from your ghost?" she asks. I say that I've only seen her once in the past two weeks and, at that time, her image was particularly faint. "I think she is moving on," I say.

"Well, of course," Maeve answers. "You've set her world to order." Then she breathes in and out before saying, "I won't be back here, you know. It's difficult and I am so tired, I'm always tired. Who would think this could happen in just two months." It is not a question and her eyes are on the lake as she talks. "You keep Eddie," she says then. "He needs one person. He needs the lake."

I don't think her children will accept this idea, but I tell Maeve I would love to have him. I think that's true, though I've never had a dog. And at this moment, I also don't believe she will not return. It seems preposterous that she would live in some facility fifteen or twenty miles inland.

There is more to say, there is always more to say between us, but the family is in a flurry of activity. Maeve gets moved into her daughter's car and the wheelchair into her trunk, Jimmy puts away the mower, inspects the property and checks all doors, and the young girls hug me as their new idol in life. Eddie watches patiently, he's such a gentleman, until he is scooted into the back seat. And they go.

Summer is turning, August on the horizon. Suddenly, the year feels old to me, as if I have lived too much in these few months. When I first found my cottage, I researched the lake here, learning it was created by melted blocks of ice from the most recent glacier, a mass that covered the northern parts of the continent seventy-five thousand years ago and broke down in great floods of water that reshaped the landscape. This lake covers fourteen thousand acres, including all inlets and bays, and overflows into a creek running many miles to the Mississippi River, which was also formed by the melting glacier. It's an ancient place. Indigenous people lived all around it, even trying to hide the whole area when settlers began nosing about in the early 1800s. Today I feel its ancient past.

In my travels, I have visited churches built on the flooded foundations of other churches, centuries of determined attempts to make a structure last, collapsed finally to the far sound of water trickling and gurgling, how deep you would never want to know. There is the story of this day, the noisy lake, the elderly friend stopping by with her family, the weight of vegetables on their vines. And there is the other story, of time and what it means. Of marvels and happenchance, of prophesy and ghosts and recurring dreams. Dying stars and undying matter. The universe shifting, expanding, collapsing, going on forever, yet finite.

I go inside my cottage still holding the coffee cup I left with this morning.

# 49

## NEWGROUND

I forgot to give Maeve the blueberry pie. I'm in a stir about this, wondering if I should bake it immediately and drive to the facility where she lives, take it piping hot with cream already whipped and hope someone has plates and silver, wondering , too, if Maeve will be in the mood for pie as she was when we sat together by the lake or if she will be bundled into a bed wanting only a watery tea to get her through the morning. Amid this fret, I hear Bo at the door.

He's on his way now. The housesitting friend is, as we speak, rearranging his meager furniture and Bo's got his things in the van, his duffel of clothes, the cardboard box of long-playing records he cannot live without, and a cooler of foodstuff to get him all the way to a far edge of the country. His radio is set to his favorite dial. His gas tank is full. And wonder of wonders, he's washed the van for its epic journey. His words.

He looks better than I have ever seen him look, which is not to say I don't like how Bo looks. I've always appreciated his ruddy skin, his long and healthy hair, the way he lumbers loosely, all joints well-oiled and ready to move. But today he about shines. "Did you cut your hair?" I ask, and it turns out he did, by a couple of inches. "For the road," he says, which makes little sense and doesn't need to, I guess. People do what they do. An uncle of mine had a complete tune-up done on his car so he could travel five miles to the nearest town for a hockey tournament. We learn young to be prepared, whatever that means to us. So Bo looks good. He's happy to be hitting the road, eager to hang out near the ocean, seemingly not at all concerned about leaving me for ten months or more.

"I'll miss you," I venture to say as we stand in the drive together examining his clean van. I do not ask him in for coffee or one more little something for the trip, because when you leave the motor racing, you are really already gone.

"Well damn, Floria, all you have to do is hop on a train, plane, or bus and head on down." He says this with a Southern twang, all fun here at his departure. He tells me there are many rooms in this house he's overseeing and that by midwinter I'll be glad to escape the northern clime. "Anytime," he insists. "Anytime."

Still, I've only known him for two months and he's the type to live in the now. Out of sight, out of mind. In all our conversations, he's never talked about a person from his past other than the wife he divorced years before. Even this friend in Port Aransas is just a guy going on a sailing trip. He has no name, no history, no story that Bo has told me. In minutes, I will join the ranks of faces in the background, on a fading horizon, another ghost in his life.

As though following my thoughts, he says I need to keep him posted on Franny Hale. "Send me word every time she shows up," he tells me. "I want to know."

Why does he want to know?

He doesn't have a ready answer, shrugs and says, "It's important, that's all. Part of the larger picture." Something he wants to understand. To make his point he texts me his phone number right this minute. "Use it," he says. "Call me whenever you want."

For a heartbeat, I think he will scoop me into a bear hug and show great affection. Instead he squeezes my arm, grins, and nods. His eyebrows arch and he keeps nodding, a secret language meant to convey something, though I can't say what. He glances a last time at the back steps he built, windows he fixed, and the garden he dug for me. He bangs on the side of his van the way a cowboy might whack the rump of his horse when ready to get going. Then that's what he does—he gets going.

I don't run after him up the graveled hill to declare undying loyalty or shout emotional goodbyes or collapse onto my steps in despair. I don't think I remember to wave. I do what I do, my way in the world, I watch and I wonder and I let the moment unfold.

Between branches of birch and white pine, I catch a glimpse of the van as it turns onto the county road and heads south. I know enough of the geography here to picture Bo's drive from the county road toward town, through town to the freeway heading first east then south and farther south, eventually taking him across the states of Iowa, Missouri, and Oklahoma before crossing the line into Texas.

When I finally move off my spot, I walk down to the dock and out to its end. I feel my grandmother's disapproval at letting Bo go so easily. Women of her day were more cunning, more strategic in their dealings with men. They had to be, of course, it was a survival skill. But to allow such a nice man to drive away like I have done would not have been in her playbook. She broke an engagement and endured two weeks crossing the Atlantic to follow my grandfather, whom she had loved since they were children. Whenever I toted young men home from college, she would assess them quickly, determine their viability, and let me know. "Looka like such a nice a boy. He eata so nice." So here she is with me on the end of the dock, head cocked to one side, whispering, *Such a nice a boy, looka like such a nice a boy.*

I sit to dangle my feet in the water. Off in the marsh between my bit of land and my neighbors to the south, I see a blue heron, its muted tone blending into the grasses and water. It takes steps closer to me with legs agile and awkward, gazing about for little fish, I guess. A solitary hunter, as Maeve observed.

Hello, I call to it, not loud enough to disturb it in any way. Just to say hello. Just to make a connection with something doing its life so near to my own. The long creature turns and looks my way, waiting to know if I will ruin its good time there in the grasses at water's edge. Then determining I am most likely harmless, it turns its eyes to the lake.

As do I.

# 50

## Come Back, I Love You, Come Back

Now August is done, and most of September. Harold tells me I need someone to get the dock ready for winter and gives me names of people who might help me, none of them Bo of course, because Bo isn't here. He did send a postcard when he first arrived in Port Aransas, an image of the beach at sunset with *I'm here!* written on the back. That is all I've heard.

Until today's cold snap, it's been a hot, muggy stretch. When Maeve's granddaughters came to visit, we opened every window wide and took a swim just before bed to cool ourselves. Eddie did too. Then he stayed for weeks, sleeping close to the north wall where he was best situated to hear Maeve if she returned next door, though she has not returned, as she told me she would not, and then a few days ago the daughter I've come to know stopped by for him. She said that if I want Eddie long term, as Maeve requested, the family is fine with that, but first he needs to go to the vet for his checkup and the youngest sweet granddaughter is bringing him to school next week for show and tell.

As Maeve always says, Eddie is good company, polite and funny. Just enough dog, not too much dog. I imagine how we will walk onto the lake once it's frozen and covered with snow, Eddie running crazy and me following behind, how he'll sit near me by the fire and alert me if anything untoward occurs around us. I'm looking forward to that. Having Eddie, though, means Maeve is not next door. She is holding on in her small space inland, calling when she remembers to call, hollering into the phone as she does to let me know how she is feeling—which is usually not too well—and what is going on just then, be it music in the lobby, a good slice of pie, or a tidbit of local news. Our conversations always end with her telling me not to lose her and me telling her I could never.

I've been over to her senior facility twice and it is a pretty place overall. I mean, efforts have been taken. Flowers grow everywhere, in pots at the door and around the building. Maeve's family keeps flowers in a vase on her dresser as well and from her window she can see a manmade pond surrounded by native grasses.

When I visit, I am introduced to staff and new friends as Floria and all Maeve's family calls me that as well. None suspect, as Bo did immediately, that this is not the name I carried through all my years until now. That name, my family name, still appears on bills from the township and the deed to this cottage, but like everything about the life I left, it continues to fade until I sometimes need a moment or more to remember who I have always been.

Maeve has stopped asking about the lake for some reason, so I have stopped reporting on the scene out here. I suspect it is easier to pretend the lake, too, has moved on, as she has, that there is nothing left for her to know now, the way my grandmother forgot to remember the mountains of her childhood until a month before she died.

Nobody talks about what will become of Maeve's house. Jimmy appears once a week to mow and we chat about weather for a minute or two, but otherwise the gray-shingled house remains in waiting. Eddie barked at it for the first two days he stayed with me, until reality sank in for him too. He continued to whimper in that direction off and on for a while and when he did, I would rub behind his ears and tell him Maeve was happy and missed him and all would be well, though of course, I have no idea if all will be well. It's what we like to say when we are considering how much might not be well, a mantra for the worried: All will be well.

And this depends on where the story ends, doesn't it? The old fable of the man whose horse broke its leg, which was bad news, until the man and his lame horse did not have to go to war, which was good news, and so on, good stumbling into bad and back to good again. Tell any story you choose, fill it with tragedy, strip off garments, destroy, march over mountains if you like, eventually it will come to some end, a last breath or scream or sigh. But is that the end?

Franny and my long-gone family speak otherwise. One way or another, the story goes on, rowing out into the middle of the lake, watching the ice layer begin to form along the shore then extend until all is frozen and the landscape gone from green to gold to white, the sky a different blue, cooler and higher, and still the story goes on—elusive, contradictory, disconcerting—but not undone.

This morning, surveying the lake from shore, I notice birds too large to be anything I expect, as though I am seeing what cannot be true, another figment of my mind. But then there is the neck of one, of two, eventually all those white tumbles raise long, thin necks of trumpeter swans. I am too far away to trouble them but not so far away I can't observe their fishing and fluffing and gliding about. Unlike the blue heron, swans are not beyond themselves in any way. They swim almost one with the water. Believe your eyes, I tell myself. Migrations happen and here is proof, the rare swan, indeed a small bevy of swans just across the bay.

I do not take the sight of rare swans as a sign exactly, but they signal a change, another season and the start of whatever will happen here in this season. I watch them until they pull themselves onto the shore over there and seem to settle in for a rest. They've come far, from Canada, I guess, and are not at their winter destination just yet. I imagine their relief, pausing to take a swim, find food, tuck into the wetland grasses where they are just now.

I once did a project in a small town on the southern coast of Nova Scotia where the only hotel gave me no peace, drunkards fighting at night and worrisome types all around. The work was challenging, the light in the office dim, the air damp and seaside chilly. To get there I needed to travel by propeller plane with a pilot younger than pilots should be. The entire harrowing journey overwhelmed me and when I finally landed back in Boston, I made my way to the oldest and most refined hotel I knew. I took off all my travel-worn clothes and sunk into an enormous tub of hot water.

This is what I am thinking, the pause in a journey, the blessed rest at the end of a tiring flight. I go back inside the cottage to grab a sweater and passing the bedroom mirror, I take a quick glance, routine for me, always trying to tame my hair into something sensible. My face is flushed from the lake breeze, my eyes still large in the wonder of swans. But something else stops me. Is it the color of my eyes? The shade of gray not my own? Or the depth beyond my depth, the wisdom beyond my wisdom, the traveler come to a journey's blessed end?

Like the swans, this is not anything I expect, but a figment, solitary and decided. I hold my breath and when I exhale, I say what I know is true but cannot be true. I look to my own image, my own presence and I say what I see:

*Franny.*

Absorbed into the timbers of this cottage, pulled through the smoke chamber of the old chimney, a sure part of my story with all the others as we spin at one thousand miles per hour on our earthly axis, returning each day to where we were the day before. Everyone coming back, as it were.

In some manner, always coming back.